SHAKUNTALA AN̶̶̶̶̶̶̶̶̶̶̶̶̶̶̶̶̶
FROM ANCIENT INDIA

Adithi Rao graduated from Smith College, USA, with a degree in Theatre, and returned to India to work as an assistant director on the Hindi film *Satya*. She went on to become a writer on a travel channel. She writes for children and adults, television and film. Her short stories have appeared in various anthology collections. *Shakuntala and Other Stories from Ancient India* and *Growing Up in Pandupur* (Young Zubaan, 2011) are her first two books.

shakuntala

and Other Timeless Tales from Ancient India

Retold by

Adithi Rao

SCHOLASTIC
New York Toronto London Auckland
Sydney New Delhi Hong Kong

For Dr Mohan Rao, for all the love he has given me

For my sister

&

my husband

This book was earlier published as *Shakuntala and Other stories from Ancient India*, Penguin, 2007

Published by Scholastic India Pvt. Ltd.
A subsidiary of Scholastic Inc., New York, 10012 (USA).
Publishers since 1920, with international operations in Canada,
Australia, New Zealand, the United Kingdom, India, and Hong Kong.

For information regarding permission, write to:
Scholastic India Pvt. Ltd.
Golf View Corporate Tower-A, 3rd Floor,
DLF Phase V, Gurgaon 122002 (India)

First edition: May 2011
Reprint: December 2011, May 2012, November 2012

ISBN-13: 978-81-8477-697-3

Printed at Aegean Offset Printers, Greater Noida

The Lexile measure of this book (800L) represents the complexity of the text. This Lexile measure—along with other characteristics of the text, such as developmental level and subject matter—helps in selecting books that best match a reader's level and goals. For more information on using Lexile measures to connect readers with text, visit www.Lexile.com.

Lexile® and the Lexile logo are trademarks of MetaMetrics, Inc., and are registered in the United States and abroad.

Contents

Abhijnanashakuntalam

Kalidasa

Placing an artist into an exact time period has been a challenge associated with many famous writers of ancient times. The Brothers Grimm might have said of Kalidasa that he lived and wrote 'in the days of yore', or even 'once upon a time'. But modern historians have tried to be a little more specific. They believe that Kalidasa belonged to either the fourth, the second or the first century BC.

Kalidasa wrote about a different world, one in which kings and sages, gods and apsaras lived together and conspired to make the world run smoothly. The Abhijnanashakuntalam, a play originally written in Sanskrit, means 'The Recognition of Shakuntala'. It is set in three worlds.

The first is the forest, filled with peace and natural beauty. In this world, Shakuntala, the heroine, is the embodiment of Nature in all its bounty and fertility. The second world is the one over which Dushyanta reigns. Fabulously decorated, replete with man-made luxuries, it is still devoid of genuine happiness. The third world is the divine one, inhabited by the holy Marica. It is the world of truth. Here Shakuntala is exonerated and rewarded for her steadfast devotion to Dushyanta.

In a sense, the three settings in Kalidasa's play are less of stage locations and more the different realms of one's conscious mind. He shows the growth of his characters through them. Dushyanta goes from being an infallible, larger-than-life hero with an eye for beautiful women, to a human man with human failings. Shakuntala, from an innocent maiden with romantic dreams in the haven of her forest, goes on to become a woman and a mother faced with the harsh realities of life. As individuals and as lovers, both grow and change immensely before they are finally reunited.

Scholars believe Abhijnanashakuntalam to be the last of Kalidasa's seven works. The original play concludes with Marica's benediction that Bharata, child of Shakuntala and Dushyanta, will go on to become the sovereign of the world. Indeed, to this day India is called Bharat, land of the descendants of Bharata.

Shakuntala

It all began in a clearing on the banks of River Malini, where King Dushyanta had come to hunt. With his bow in hand, he looked regal and handsome as he raced along in his swift chariot in pursuit of a deer.

'Stop!'

Dushyanta drew his chariot to a halt and looked towards the sound in surprise.

'O king, that deer belongs to sage Kanva. It does not deserve to die.'

It was an ascetic who spoke.

Dushyanta got down from his chariot and bowed to the hermit. 'Forgive me, holy one. I will hunt here no more. Only, tell me where I can find the revered sage. I wish to pay my respects to him before returning home.'

'He is away on pilgrimage.' The ascetic was impressed with Dushyanta's humility. Few kings would have taken a refusal of this kind so good naturedly, least of all one of Dushyanata's fame and power. The ascetic blessed him saying, 'May you father a son who will rule the world.'

When the ascetic left, Dushyanta looked about him and was struck by the beauty of his surroundings.

'Let me enter this hermitage of sage Kanva and rest here,' he thought. 'This is a different world! The trees are greener, the bird song sweeter, the waters of the stream more blue! How the breeze is weaving silence into melody ...'

Suddenly, there was the sound of female voices. Dushyanta saw three girls appear, two of them giggling and chattering as they picked flowers. But he was standing near a clump of trees and was almost hidden from their view.

The third girl was different. She was so ethereally beautiful and delicate that Dushyanta was captivated! He had never seen a girl like her before. She seemed to float along the ground rather than walk, as she followed her companions into the clearing.

At the rustling from the bushes, the first two girls stopped chatting and turned around. They saw the king's wistful eyes gazing upon their lovely friend.

'Look!' whispered one to the other. 'A stranger!'

They beckoned to Dushyanta and he emerged.

The third girl glanced up from her task of watering the mandara saplings. At the sight of Dushyanta, handsome and tall, she felt suddenly shy and breathless.

'She is agitated at the sight of me! She is so delicate I can see the quickening of her pulse at the base of her lovely throat,' thought Dushyanta. He said, 'Fair maidens, may I be so forward as to ask who you are?'

'His lips ask for all three of our names, but his eyes betray his true interest,' whispered one girl to the other.

With a knowing smile, she replied, 'This is Shakuntala, the daughter of sage Kanva. We are Priyamvada and Anasuya, her companions.'

'I am honoured to make your acquaintance. But tell me, how could the great sage, vowed to celibacy for all times, have had a child?'

'She is not his natural born child, but the child of the apsara Menaka and sage Vishwamitra. Vishwamitra was engaged in harsh penance, and the gods became nervous. Lord Indra sent the lovely Menaka to distract the sage, and Shakuntala was born of their union. But Vishwamitra returned to his penance, and after the birth of the child, Menaka was summoned back to her celestial home. Sage Kanva found Shakuntala abandoned as an infant and raised her as his own. She is the apple of his eye, the light of his life. But I have spoken too much already. And who, sir, are you? We hear King Dushyanta is in these parts. Are you of his entourage?'

Dushyanta started to correct her, but changed his mind. 'I am.'

'Then you must come and partake of our hospitality. Sage Kanva will be sorry to have missed you. For surely, had he been here,' and Anasuya threw a meaningful glance at the blushing Shakuntala, 'he would have honoured you with his most precious treasure.'

'Anasuya!' cried Shakuntala, embarrassed, and started to walk away.

'Please,' called Dushyanta, before he could stop himself, 'Don't leave.'

'Won't you come with us?' asked Priyamvada quickly. Shakuntala's steps faltered, waiting for his response.

'I'm afraid I have delayed too much already.'

'Then we must go our way, sir, for we are expected at the hermitage,' said Priyamvada, as Shakuntala's slender shoulders drooped with disappointment.

That night, Dushyanta could not sleep. Thoughts of Shakuntala filled him with longing. The hours crawled slowly by, and it was as if that night had no morning. He was troubled by a hundred questions.

He gazed at the moon, as if it had the answers. 'O Moon,' he said, 'does she love me as I love her? Will she ever be mine? Give me some cause to hope.'

But the moon stared mutely back at him.

The next morning, two disciples of Kanva arrived at Dushyanta's tent in the forest.

'Blessings upon you, O king!'

'Welcome, holy sirs.' Dushyanta rose from his seat respectfully.

'The residents of the hermitage of Kanva request your presence at the sacred rites. Each time we perform them the demons do everything they can to disrupt the ceremonies. So far only the powerful presence of Father Kanva has stopped them. But now, in his absence, these demons will surely succeed. Please protect us.'

'It will be my honour,' replied Dushyanta, reaching for his bow.

Everybody at the hermitage was anxiously awaiting the arrival of King Dushyanta. They feared the demons would strike before he could come. They were also eager to set eyes upon the great monarch, whose reputation for his handsomeness, intelligence and courage were well-known. Shakuntala waited with the rest, but without enthusiasm. She was preoccupied with thoughts of a member of that very king's entourage (or so she thought!), the handsome stranger she had met the previous day.

So imagine her astonishment when she saw her stranger riding up in a chariot that bore the flag of King Dushyanta! Imagine her joy when she discovered that he was none other than that great king; her pride when he crushed fearsome demons as if they were ants beneath his feet!

Overcome by emotion, Shakuntala ran away, and Dushyanta's restless gaze searched for her in vain.

When the ceremonies were over, Shakuntala and her friends returned to the clearing. Dushyanta was there too, resting behind a tree, although they did not know it. Priyamvada and Anasuya could speak of nothing but the charming stranger's true identity, but Shakuntala was agitated.

'What is the matter, Shakuntala? Today even the little fawn has failed to make you smile.'

'I'm deeply troubled.'

'Why?'

Dushyanta strained forward, his heart beating rapidly.

Embarrassed, Shakuntala spoke softly, 'The moment I set eyes on Dushyanta, I fell in love with him. What do I do? How do I get him to love me in return before he leaves forever?'

Hearing these words, Dushyanta could not contain his joy. He stepped out from behind the tree crying, 'My love!' and drew Shakuntala into his arms. Priyamvada and Anasuya left quickly as the king slipped his signet ring upon her finger and bent to kiss her ...

The marriage between Dushyanta and Shakuntala took place by the Gandharva rites. The union between them was the only ceremony that served to bind them together as man and wife. Shortly after, his duties as king forced Dushyanta to return to his palace. He promised to come back for Shakuntala soon. Shakuntala's heart grew heavier with each passing day. She was pregnant with Dushyanta's child but that did little to lift her spirits. Priyamvada and Anasuya watched over her, eagerly awaiting the return of Kanva.

However, it was not Kanva who arrived first but sage Durvasa. Feared for his terrible temper, even the gods quaked at the prospect of incurring Durvasa's wrath. Whether a blessing or a curse, his every utterance unfailingly came true. Kunti, the wife of Pandu, had once served Durvasa with great diligence. Well pleased, he had taught her a mantra through which she conceived Karna and the five mighty Pandavas.

Shakuntala was not so fortunate. Entirely lost in thoughts of her Dushyanta, she did not hear Durvasa when he stood at the door of the hermitage and called out, 'Here I am!' expecting every hospitality that was due to a guest.

When greeted by her absent-minded silence, Durvasa's temper flared. 'What insolence to ignore a guest, and that too one of my status! May the person whose thoughts occupy you so completely forget you forever!'

These words, too, went by Shakuntala's ears unheard. But Anasuya and Priyamvada, returning from the forest at that moment, heard and were horrified. They dropped their baskets and ran after him, begging him to spare their friend.

At long last Durvasa relented. 'I cannot retract my words,' he said, 'But I can soften them to this—should your friend produce some ornament given to her by her husband, he shall recognise her again.'

Thanking him profusely, Anasuya and Priyamvada returned to Shakuntala.

'Let us not tell her about this.'

'Yes. Knowing of this curse will only agitate her further in this delicate condition.'

So the two said nothing.

Meanwhile Kanva had set out for home after completing his pilgrimage. It took him many days of walking, and as he neared the forest of his hermitage his heart lifted with joy at the thought of seeing Shakuntala again. As he passed through the forest, he heard the trees whispering. But when he stopped to inquire they fell instantly silent.

'My friends,' he said gently, 'you are inhabitants of the hermitage of which I am father. By that right you are my children and need not be afraid of me. If you have something to say, speak freely.'

'Father,' they replied, 'our sister Shakuntala has secretly married King Dushyanta, and is now carrying his child.'

Kanva was happy, 'This is good news! I myself could have found nobody worthier of my precious child!' Blessing the trees for being the bearers of such good tidings, Kanva hurried home.

On arriving, he began immediately to make the necessary arrangements to send Shakuntala to her husband's home. In a few days' time the preparations were made, and it was with a heavy heart that Kanva blessed Shakuntala, 'May your husband honour you with the status of Primary Queen. May you bear a son to whom the whole world will bow.'

As they clung tearfully to their friend, Priyamvada and Anasuya whispered, 'Shakuntala, listen carefully. Should, by some twist of fate, King Dushyanta fail to recognise you, show him the signet ring he put on your finger the day he married you.'

Thus Shakuntala's journey from the hermitage to her husband's home began. Accompanied by Kanva's two disciples, she crossed rivers and lakes and forests until she reached the palace of King Dushyanta.

Inside the palace, Dushyanta was listening to the

beautiful strains of the veena being played in the chamber beyond his quarters.

'This music fills my heart with yearning. But what is the reason for my sadness? I cannot seem to remember, and yet I cannot shake it off.'

A chamberlain entered. 'Your Majesty, two hermits have arrived with a message from sage Kanva. They are accompanied by a woman.'

'Show them in.'

Receiving them with honour, Dushyanta glanced at Shakuntala frequently, struck by her beauty. But he neither recognised nor addressed her.

Shakuntala grew anxious. 'My worst fears are coming true!' she thought. 'My husband looks at me but shows no joy or recognition. There is none of the old love in his eyes. Can it be that he will reject me?'

Meanwhile the disciples conveyed Kanva's greetings to the king in his own words:

We are ascetics, rich in self-restraint,
And you are a king of exalted lineage.
This daughter of an ascetic has loved you spontaneously,
And of her own free will.
Accept her, then, as your consort, worth equal esteem
As your other wives;
Whether you love her above them depends on her fate;
The bride's father has no right to demand it.

This was Kanva's entreaty to Dushyanta to accept Shakuntala and her unborn child into their rightful home.

But the king was surprised. 'There must be some mistake. She is a beautiful woman with exceptional grace, not one a man can easily forget, especially not a husband. And yet I do not recall ever seeing her before. Surely I would have some memory of it had I married her! No, she is another's wife, carrying another's child.'

Shakuntala was horrified. She looked at her husband in stunned silence. Then, suddenly recalling her friends' parting words about showing Dushyanta the signet ring, she frantically felt about her person ... and found the ring gone!

'This is a cruel blow from fate indeed! It must have fallen into the lake I bathed in on my way here. There is no room for me in my husband's home. Slighted and rejected, I must return to my father. Brothers, come, let us hear no more of this. Let us leave at once.'

But the disciples of Kanva replied, 'Sister, yours was a marriage made in secret. Denied by this man you claim is your husband, it is not fitting that you should return with us. Besides, if indeed what you say is true, your fate now rests in his hands, for a husband's authority over his wife is absolute. Thus we are forced to leave without you.'

The disciples set out for the hermitage once more. Shocked by their manner, angered and grieved by Dushyanta's faithlessness, Shakuntala, too, left the palace.

As he watched her go, Dushyanta said to himself, 'True that I have no memory of marrying this girl. Yet the ache in my heart tells me that there may be some truth to her words ...'

The seasons changed and life in the palace went on as before. Then one day, as Dushyanta was holding court, there was a commotion outside the palace doors.

'You thief! Where did you find this ring? Confess!' came the voice of the police chief.

'Honourable sir, I am just a humble fisherman. Yesterday I caught a very large fish. When I cut open its belly, I found this ring. The kotwal saw it in my hand and arrested me.'

'That's a tall story indeed. This is a matter for the king.'

The fisherman was dragged before Dushyanta and the whole story was told again for his benefit. Dushyanta held out his hand and the police chief carefully placed the ring in his palm. Dushyanta's eyes fell upon the gem, heavily set in gold. He saw the coat of arms of his dynasty etched into the stone. His signet ring! The memories come flooding back, staggering him. Shakuntala! Their wedding day; the promises he made and never kept! And most of all, the love they had shared.

With a wordless cry he half-rose from his throne and collapsed back into it, dropping his head into his hands and weeping with sorrow and guilt.

From that day on, Dushyanta knew no peace. His tortured days and sleepless nights were spent in frantic search for his beloved wife. Messengers were sent far and wide to look for

Shakuntala, but the end of each search only brought the same disappointing report: 'She is nowhere to be found.'

Shakuntala, the light of Dushyanta's life, had disappeared, leaving behind only darkness. Here was Dushyanta, mighty ruler, with palaces and armies at his disposal. Yet he forgot the meaning of happiness. Each day dawned clear, but brought with it no light. Despair, only despair and guilt and hopelessness. As time went by, he grew unhappy and ill from grief. In spite of the many futile months of searching, his heart could not resign itself to its loss.

Then Matali, trusted envoy of Lord Indra, came to see Dushyanta.

'O mighty king. My Lord Indra sends me here with a plea for help.'

Roused from his morose state, Dushyanta replied, 'Command me, friend.'

'There is a race of giants that is destined to die at your hands alone. The Lord asks you to fulfil this duty that Destiny has charged you with.'

'I will come this instant.' Mounting Indra's chariot, Dushyanta left with Matali for the celestial regions.

In the terrible battle that ensued, Dushyanta fought alone. It was the strength of a single bow pitted against the force of a hundred fearsome giants. As each mighty giant fell under Dushyanta's relentless arrows, the earth shook and trembled. The battle raged for many days and many nights, victory oscillating from this side to that, but never firmly planting its feet on either ground. Yet, who can change what Destiny has already decided? In the end the giants were vanquished. The gods were overjoyed!

On the journey from the heavens back to Dushyanta's palace, Dushyanta and Matali halted at the hermitage of the great sage Marica.

'I must pay my respects to His Holiness, Matali. Such an opportunity for blessings must not be lost,' said Dushyanta. Descending from the chariot, he prostrated himself before the sage and his consort, Aditi.

'May you be blessed with a son who will rule the world,' they said. In that same instant there was a commotion from behind. Dushyanta got to his feet and turned around. There he saw a little boy, radiant as the moon, playing with a lion cub. Hovering close were two ladies doing everything in their power to get the child to leave the cub alone. Their efforts proved futile.

'How fearless he is. How strong and brave. My heart is drawn towards this child,' thought Dushyanta.

In the tussle between lion cub and child, the boy's amulet fell on the ground. Dushyanta bent to retrieve it just as the ladies rushed forward.

'No!' they cried, 'Don't touch it!'

Too late! Dushyanta held the amulet out to them, and they stepped back with widened eyes.

'It is he!'

'The boy's father!'

Taking a step forward, Dushyanta asked urgently, 'What? What did you say?'

'That amulet was put on the child's arm by His Holiness Marica as a talisman against danger. If it falls, only the boy or his parents may pick it up without being killed the instant they touch it.'

At that moment, a woman emerged from the hermitage calling to the boy in loving tones, 'Bharata! Come, it is time for your meal.'

Dushyanta turned around and stood still at the sight of the woman. The same loveliness! The same gentle, ethereal beauty, only made more poignant by sorrow and motherhood.

'Shakuntala!'

Shakuntala came out of the hut, hardly daring to believe her eyes. 'It is my husband! He calls me by name. Could my fate have relented towards me at last?'

Dushyanta ran to Shakuntala, dropping to his knees before her, begging her forgiveness. The boy approached them, and Dushyanta gathered him into his loving embrace.

'Don't blame yourself, Dushyanta,' said Marica. 'You are not guilty of the sin you beg forgiveness for. You were the victim of Durvasa's curse. Now return home with your wife and child, restore them to their rightful positions, and rule in glory for many years to come.'

And as every utterance of the holy Marica invariably came to pass, so also did this prediction, spoken in blessing.

Mrichchakatika

Shudraka

Shudraka's Mrichchakatika *was probably staged in Ujjaini, a prosperous kingdom of ancient India, some two thousand years ago. Shudraka is not among the foremost Sanskrit playwrights, but* Mrichchakatika *is one of the more popular and timeless works of literature. It is known for its down-to-earth, humorous and vivacious depiction of everyday life and society.*

Mrichchakatika *translates from Sanskrit as 'The Clay Cart'. There are two plots to the play—the love between Charudatta and the courtesan Vasantasena, and the growing political unrest in Ujjaini. Unlike Kalidasa and other famous writers of that era, Shudraka writes about the common man.* Mrichchakatika *deals with the struggles of the commoner, the interaction between the classes of society (viz. Brahmins, Kshatriyas, Vaishyas and Shudras), and the triumph of democracy (where the people incite a successful rebellion against their tyrannical king and replace him with one from their own ranks).*

It is interesting to note that Shudraka has the title of 'King' attached to his name. Some historians believe King Shudraka to be the founder of the Andhrabhritya Dynasty (200 BC). Mrichchakatika, as far as we know, might be Shudraka's only piece of writing.

Shudraka's heroine is not a queen or a princess, but a courtesan. In those times, courtesans ranked fairly low in the social order. Mrichchakatika is realistic and approachable because it blurs the lines between good and bad, uses simple people as its protagonists, and entirely avoids using divine intervention to take the plot forward.

The Little Clay Cart

'Stop, lovely maiden! I beg you to stop!'

The courtesan Vasantasena turned her head and realised in a panic that Samsthanaka and his companions were gaining on her. With one last surge of effort she forced her tired legs to move faster.

'Why do you abuse your lotus-like feet so? Stop!' cried Samsthanaka, gasping for breath. 'O charioteer, O friend Vita, tell my beloved not to run from me,' he added beseechingly to his companions.

Taking pity on Samsthanaka, Vita and the charioteer Sthavaraka chased after the fleeing Vasantasena and caught her by the hem of her garment. Desperately she swung around, knowing herself to be cornered. Behind her was a deadend. Only an old house stood there.

Samsthanaka, obese and winded, came panting up, bent double with his efforts.

'Oh!' he gasped, 'Oh! Oh! Oh!'

'Sir,' cried Sthavaraka, running to him in alarm, 'are you alright?'

After leaning his considerable weight on the puny Sthavaraka and catching his breath, Samsthanaka straightened up and pushed him away. 'You fool! What makes you think I need your help? I, the fittest and most youthful of men, desired by every maiden in Ujjaini? I, brother-in-law of the great King Palaka! Keep your hands off me, you son-of-a-slave!'

Despite her terror, Vasantasena knew a moment of incredulous surprise as she heard Samsthanaka describe himself so. Surely, a fatter, more ill-proportioned fellow did not exist in the kingdom? But in the next instant her fear returned, for Samsthanaka began to advance towards her with his arms flung out.

'Pallavi!' cried Vasantasena, looking about her desperately. 'Madhavika! Help me!'

'She is calling to her bodyguards!' panicked Samsthanaka, hastily retreating.

'Those are not the names of bodyguards; she is calling her maids!' said Vita, shaking his head in exasperation.

'Oh well, in that case ...' and Samsthanaka came for Vasantasena again.

'I have been separated from my maids. I must protect myself from this ridiculous fool somehow,' thought Vasantasena in terror as Samsthanaka grabbed her by her hair.

Trying to distract him, Vasantasena said humbly, 'Sirs, why have you cornered me? Do you hope to take my ornaments?'

'In a manner of speaking,' said Vita. 'He hopes to win you, the brightest ornament in Ujjaini.'

'Surely a man of my beauty and wealth deserves, no, *commands* the love of a lowly courtesan like yourself!' said Samsthanaka pompously.

'Indeed no!' exclaimed the lady furiously. 'For I already love another man!'

'That penniless beggar Charudatta, I hear,' said Samsthanaka. Laughing derisively, he pointed out to his companions, 'There is his house now, that old dilapidated one with its walls peeling off!'

Vasantasena's heart lightened. 'So this is my beloved's house! I shall seek his protection.' Without waiting another second she quickly turned and disappeared into the darkness. Only Vita saw her leave.

That foolish Samsthanaka gave her the information she needed to escape.

'How strange Fate is, to favour a worthless tyrant like him and turn its back on the worthy Charudatta. Never mind, I will not say a word. Even a courtesan deserves better than this idiot,' thought Vita.

When Samsthanaka swung around to make another grab at Vasantasena, his hand closed over thin air. 'Where has she gone? Friends, my Vasantasena has disappeared into the night!' he whined.

'If I have to put up with him much longer I shall kill him,' mumbled Vita. Assuring Samsthanaka that they would resume their search in the morning, he led him away quickly. Samsthanaka was actually quite relieved as he was rather afraid of the dark.

Meanwhile, Vasantasena entered the gates of Charudatta's home and quietly made her way through the courtyard. Then she heard a voice saying, 'O Poverty, my constant companion, I worry about you. Where will you go once death has taken me from you? Maitreya, what respect does a man like me get when Luck has forsaken me?'

'That is Charudatta's voice!' thought Vasantasena. 'I shall not interrupt, but hide here and listen.'

'Friend,' replied Maitreya, 'do not say so. Your wealth was not lost but given away to the needy. You are not alone. You have honour, reputation and the goodwill of all Ujjaini!'

'Maitreya is the one steady friend who did not forsake my Charudatta when he lost his fortunes. How true and honest his words are!' thought Vasantasena.

Just then a gust of wind blew out the oil lamp, throwing the courtyard and Vasantasena into darkness. Maitreya hurried away to light it. Taking advantage of the opportunity, Vasantasena stepped into the room.

'Radhanika,' said Charudatta, mistaking her for the maid. 'Take Rohasena inside. It is getting chilly here. Take my cloak and cover him with it.' Pulling off the cloak from around his shoulders, he threw it to Vasantasena. With joy she caught it and drew it about herself. With the scent and warmth of his body still on it, for a moment she imagined that she was standing in his arms.

'Radhanika? Why won't you answer me?' came Charudatta's voice again. At that moment the flame from the lamp brightened the room again.

'Sir, here I am. Did you want something?' asked Radhanika, entering the inner courtyard along with Maitreya.

'What! You, here? Then who ...?' asked Charudatta, looking around him in confusion. When his eyes fell on Vasantasena he was horrified.

'Good lady, I have polluted you with my cloak! Forgive me, it was done in ignorance.'

'Rather, say blessed me with it, sir,' replied Vasantasena, still clutching the cloak to her body and shyly lowering her eyes.

Puzzled, Charudatta opened his mouth. Before he could speak, Maitreya said, 'She is the courtesan Vasantasena. All Ujjaini knows that she is in love with you!'

Vasantasena quickly raised her anxious eyes to Charudatta's face and then dropped them again. As he looked into her bent face, Charudatta felt a surge of reciprocal love. Yet, when he spoke, his words were dispassionate. 'She must forget about me, for my fortunes will not permit me to win her love.'

'It is said that she has rejected the powerful Samsthanaka time and again for you,' put in Maitreya.

'He is right, my lord. Wealth and power no longer impresses me. You have already won me by your merits.'

Vasantasena spoke with her heart in her eyes, and Charudatta was touched.

Gently he questioned, 'To what do we owe the honour of your visit?'

Quickly searching her mind, Vasantasena came up with a plan. 'Sir, some evil men have been chasing me. They are after this ornament.' She removed her necklace and held it out to Charudatta. 'I request you to keep it safe for me until I come back for it, because my house is a good distance away and there are thieves about at this time of the night.'

'My lady, forgive me. This is not a house that can be entrusted with such a precious ornament,' replied Charudatta, indicating the broken and peeling walls.

'It is not in this house, but in its owner that I place my trust.'

Charudatta could not refuse such a plea. Nodding, he said, 'Maitreya, take the ornament. It must be returned to this lady safely.'

'Now I shall have other opportunities of meeting him,' thought Vasantasena happily.

'Thank you, sir,' she said aloud. 'Now I must take your leave.'

'Maitreya, will you escort her home?' asked Charudatta of his friend.

'Indeed no. What sort of protection is a puny fellow like me to a beautiful woman in the dead of the night?'

'Then I will escort her myself.'

Vasantasena was overjoyed. The two of them left the house together. As they made their way through the darkened streets to her mansion, they did not speak but stole glances at each other. But when they reached her gate and Charudatta said quietly, 'Madam, here is your home,' something in his voice told Vasantasena that he had fallen in love with her too.

The next day Vasantasena refused to go down for morning prayers. Instead she sat in her room and poured her heart out to Madanika. Madanika was a slave girl, but Vasantasena valued her as her closest and dearest friend.

'My mistress has been struck by Kama's arrow!'

'How can you tell?' asked Vasantasena.

'You are absent-minded and your speech is disconnected. Your eyes are soft and filled with dreams. There can be only one explanation for this! My only question is, who is the worthy gentleman?' asked Madanika.

'Need you ask?'

'Is it a king?'

'No.'

'The son of a king, then?'

'No.'

'A wealthy merchant who has amassed a great fortune?'

'Indeed no!'

'Then tell me who.'

'Madanika, you visited the shrine of Kamadeva with me ...'

'I know! It is Charudatta, the man we saw at the temple.

The richest man in Ujjaini!'

'He has lost his fortune,' said Vasantasena sadly.

'My lady, I meant honour and merit, the only fortunes a man may take with him out of this world.'

Touched by her words, Vasantasena embraced Madanika. Just then they heard a commotion outside.

'What is it?' cried Vasantasena in alarm.

'Wait, my lady. I will see.' Madanika ran to the window and looked out into the street below. She saw a man running as if from death. Spotting the open gates of Vasantasena's mansion, he ran inside. His pursuers—two men—followed a little distance behind. At the gate they stopped and looked around.

'He has disappeared!' said one man, agitated.

'That rascal got away! I shall kill him when I find him!' cried the other angrily.

'My lady,' said Madanika, 'there is a man downstairs who seeks your refuge.'

'I'll go down at once.'

The two girls went down the stairs and to the courtyard below, where they found a terrified fellow looking about him desperately.

'Don't be afraid,' said Vasantasena gently. 'Tell me what the trouble is.'

'Madam, I am Samvahaka, a gambler who has lost his fortune. Now I am unable to pay my dues. There are two men outside, the gamester and the master of the gambling house. They are after me to collect the ten gold mudras that I owe them. I am a poor man and the money I lost today was the last of it. If they catch me I am as good as dead. Please protect me!'

Thinking quickly, Vasantasena removed a gold bracelet from her wrist. 'Madanika, give this to the men outside.'

Madanika went out and returned shortly. 'My lady, the men have accepted the bracelet and gone away satisfied.' Then with a laugh she added, 'They have sent a message to this gentleman telling him that he may come back and throw the dice at their gaming house again anytime he wishes to!'

Samvahaka folded his hands to Vasantasena. There were tears of gratitude in his eyes. 'I shall remain indebted to you forever.'

'No such promise is required, sir. Go in peace,' replied Vasantasena.

'Madam,' he said, 'your kindness saved the life of a worthless fellow. Please don't think it is in vain. I spent my days and nights among liars and cheats until I became one myself. But your goodness and generosity has shown me another side of humanity. I will never gamble again. I will join the Buddhist order and become a monk. Know that you are responsible for converting a bad man into a good one. May god bless you!'

Samvahaka left the house.

That night Charudatta and Maitreya returned home from a music concert, tired. As they entered the courtyard of Charudatta's home, the charioteer came forward and handed the casket containing Vasantasena's necklace to Maitreya.

'I shall use this as a pillow for my head,' said Maitreya. 'That way no one will be able to lay a hand on it.'

The two of them quickly settled down to sleep. When the moon had set and all was still, a figure detached itself from the darkness and approached the house of Charudatta.

'Ah, a dilapidated house with crumbling walls. Shouldn't be difficult to break into,' thought Sarvilaka.

Sarvilaka was not a thief. At least not by profession. He was a decent fellow who was down on his luck, and desperately in love with Madanika. 'I don't know of any other way to buy her freedom and make her mine,' he thought.

Had Madanika known of her lover's plans she would have died rather than allow him to turn thief for her sake. Using the rules for breaking an entry as described in ancient books, he penetrated the outer wall of Charudatta's home and made his way into the inner quadrangle. He made little noise, but the sharp ears of the sleeping Maitreya picked up something. Raising his head sleepily, he said, 'Charudatta, there seems to be a thief about. Here, take the casket and keep it with you.'

Charudatta was deeply asleep and did not hear him. But Sarvilaka, who had just entered the room, did.

'What luck!' he thought. 'This fellow is making my work easy!' He took the casket that Maitreya was holding out and quickly left the house.

In the morning the hole in the outer wall was discovered, and pandemonium reigned in Charudatta's house. Coupled with the missing casket, there was only one explanation everyone could come up with.

'I thought the fellow was you!' mourned Maitreya for the hundredth time.

'Never mind, friend. It was a natural mistake,' replied Charudatta, trying to appear calm.

Inside he was in utter despair. 'The loss of my fortunes I could bear with equanimity,' he thought. 'But this stain on my reputation is a calamity. Now all the world will think that I stole Vasantasena's necklace. And what of that girl who placed her trust in me? How to face her? In one night I have lost my peace of mind, my reputation, and the woman I love. Surely there can be no poorer man in Ujjaini than I, not even the poverty-stricken Charudatta of yesterday!' On the surface, however, he remained calm.

Meanwhile Sarvilaka rushed off to Vasantasena's mansion, holding the casket in his hand. When he reached he found Madanika alone, dusting the priceless works of art that decorated the lower quarters.

'What brings you here?' asked Madanika formally. But the glow in her eyes betrayed her love for Sarvilaka.

'Madanika, I have come to buy your freedom!'

'Indeed? You who have little money, have you suddenly come into favour with the king?' teased Madanika.

'Don't tease me, my love. For it is only the wicked and the corrupt who come into favour with our king. But take heart! The prophecy says that my noble friend Aryaka the cowherd will soon become ruler of Ujjaini,' cried Sarvilaka, happily.

'But that doesn't explain how you came into money,' said Madanika, bringing him back to the subject.

'My dear, I'm afraid to tell you, for you will frown upon my means. Yet I beg you to remember that it is only my love for you that prompted me to become a ...'

'A what?' asked Madanika fearfully. 'O Sarvilaka, tell me quickly, for my heart is in terror!'

'A thief.'

As he said these words he opened the casket and displayed Vasantasena's necklace inside. Madanika took one look at it and fainted. Rushing to her side, Sarvilaka anxiously sprinkled water from a flower vase on her eyes.

She sat up slowly and despair claimed her. 'Sarvilaka, what have you done in the name of love? You have stolen from the best of men, and what you have stolen is the very necklace my gentle mistress handed over to him for safekeeping. And now you hope to redeem me against this necklace. Do you see what a mess you have made?'

Sarvilaka was horrified. 'What do I do now, Madanika?'

Thinking quickly, Madanika came up with a plan. 'Listen carefully. You must go to my mistress and tell her that Charudatta has sent you to return this casket on his behalf. As for my freedom ... we will have to forget about that now.' These last words Madanika spoke softly, sadly. Sarvilaka came forward and took her in his arms.

Little did the lovers know that Vasantasena had come out onto the landing and quietly heard every word they had spoken.

Meanwhile, Dhuta, the chaste wife of Charudatta, sent for Maitreya.

'Madam, command me,' said Maitreya as he stood before her with folded hands.

'You are my husband's one true friend, which is why I am entrusting you with this task. Sir, I heard about the theft of the necklace. I know that my husband's reputation is dearer to him than his own life. He is my life, and his honour is my deepest concern. Without it neither he nor I can exist.' She removed a beautiful necklace from around her neck and held it out to Maitreya, 'Please ask my husband to give this in place of the stolen necklace.'

'Is this necessary?' asked Maitreya sadly. 'You have lost all your ornaments to ill-fortune. You, who were once adorned in silks and gold like the Goddess Lakshmi, today have only this one last necklace. It is studded with precious stones, and its value far exceeds that of the stolen one. Please do not part with it.'

'Sir,' said Dhuta with finality, 'kindly do as I request or I shall have to find someone else to take this necklace to your friend.'

Resignedly Maitreya accepted his charge and left the quarters. When he gave it to Charudatta with Dhuta's message, Charudatta's eyes filled with tears. Staring down at the necklace which he had seen on his beloved wife so many times, he said softly, 'How can a man consider himself unlucky when he has a wife like mine?' Looking up, Charudatta said, 'Friend Maitreya, be so kind as to deliver this to Vasantasena in her home. Explain to her that her necklace was stolen and beg her to accept this replacement with my humblest apologies.'

Maitreya took the ornament and left the house.

At Vasantasena's home another drama was unfolding. When Sarvilaka and Madanika finished talking about the theft of the necklace, Vasantasena made her presence known. Going according to Madanika's plan, Sarvilaka stepped forward and greeted Vasantasena with folded hands. He handed over the casket to her and said, 'Madam, Charudatta has sent me to return this to you.'

Not wanting to let on that she knew the truth, Vasantasena accepted the casket graciously, asking Sarvilaka to convey her thanks to his master. As he made to leave, stealing one last fleeting look at his beloved's face, Vasantasena stopped him.

'It is customary to reward a messenger. I have yet to give you yours.'

At this, Sarvilaka dropped his eyes in shame, knowing that he did not deserve this kindness.

'Here is your reward,' said Vasantasena, drawing Madanika by the hand and gently pushing her towards Sarvilaka.

Sarvilaka's eyes darted from one maiden's face to the other in disbelief. Madanika only looked at Vasantasena in wonderment. Smiling at her beloved friend, Vasantasena said to Madanika, 'Silly girl, we have grown up together. Did you really think I did not know your feelings?'

'But to take her free of cost ...' began Sarvilaka.

'Madanika is priceless to me. No amount of money would compensate me for her loss. So the only payment I ask is that you keep her happy always.'

'I promise you that a thousand times over!' cried Sarvilaka. 'And I thank you again and again for your generosity!'

Madanika said nothing. She only embraced Vasantasena with tears in her eyes.

As Sarvilaka and Madanika made their way out of the city, they heard a commotion.

'What is all the noise about?' Sarvilaka asked a passerby.

'King Palaka heard about the prophecy and has captured Aryaka and thrown him into prison! Our last hope of being saved from the tyranny of Palaka is dwindling!'

'What?' cried Sarvilaka. 'The future king of Ujjaini imprisoned? This cannot be. I must hurry and collect a group of loyal followers and incite a rebellion. That is the only way to overthrow Palaka now!'

Turning to Madanika he said, 'Dearest, go ahead to my parent's home and I will join you there when my work is done.'

'Come back soon,' replied Madanika.

They embraced and went their different ways.

Vasantasena was resting in her quarters, lost in thoughts of Charudatta, when she heard the sound of voices in the street below. Looking out of her window she saw Maitreya talking to the gatekeeper. A few moments later the gates of the mansion were opened and Maitreya disappeared through them.

'Wonderful! Perhaps his coming here might give me an opportunity of a meeting with my beloved again!' Vasantasena ran down to greet Maitreya.

Maitreya looked around at the lavish surroundings. His thirsty eyes, now unused to the trappings of wealth, were soaking up the scene greedily. Impressed though he was by Vasantasena's obvious affluence and good taste, he began to feel jealous and resentful.

So when Vasantasena came down and received him graciously, his praise of her home was lavish but marked with derision. Luckily she was too eager to hear Charudatta's message to notice his manner.

'Madam, my friend has asked you to forgive his inability to protect what you so trustingly left in his care. In its stead he begs that you accept this necklace.'

'Sir, I thank you and the noble Charudatta. Please tell him that I intend to pay him a visit this evening to thank him in person.'

Vasantasena did not give away the fact that she already

had in her possession the original necklace. 'I will disclose this secret later, and to Charudatta only,' she thought.

But Maitreya's hardened heart chose to take another view of the matter. 'This woman does not truly love my friend,' he thought. One look at the necklace would reveal that its worth is far greater than the one she left with him. Yet she is happy to accept this one in its place, knowing full well how poor he is. How different she is from the good Dhuta. Well, after all she is only a courtesan.

When he returned to Charudatta's house, Maitreya poured out his misgivings about Vasantasena. But Charudatta, who listened patiently, only smiled.

The evening was cloudy. Vasantasena anxiously looked out of her carriage at the overcast sky. Just as she reached the home of Charudatta the overcast sky finally gave way and the rain came down in torrents.

'Lady,' said Charudatta once they had exchanged greetings, 'I'm afraid you will not be able to leave this house tonight. The rains are exceedingly heavy. I will have a room prepared for you.'

He went away to instruct the servants to prepare the best room in the house for Vasantasena. While he was gone, Vasantasena wandered about the outer quarters, amusing herself with the murals on the walls, faded with time but still beautiful, testifying to the wealth that had now passed it by. Suddenly she heard a child crying out from the next room, 'No! I don't want this one! Take it away!'

Hurrying to the source of the noise, she found a beautiful little boy. His nurse was trying in vain to cajole him to play with a little clay cart that was lying on the floor.

'What is the matter?' asked Vasantasena, gently drawing the boy to her. He was definitely Rohasena, Charudatta's little son. The resemblance was unmistakable.

'Madam, he refuses to play with his toy,' replied the harassed nurse.

'Well, so what? Bring him another,' said Vasantasena.

'But he has no other.'

'Oh!' said Vasantasena. 'Son, why won't you play with this cart?' she asked the child.

'Because it is made of clay! I want one made of gold.'

'Then here,' said Vasantasena, removing some of her ornaments and putting them into the cart. 'Now it is a cart carrying gold. Does that make you happy?'

Rohasena smiled. 'Who is this lady?' he asked his nurse.

'You may know me as your mother.'

'That cannot be. My mother wears no jewels,' replied Rohasena with finality.

'Then let me remove the rest of my ornaments as well.' Doing so she put them into the cart along with the others and stood before the boy. 'Now will you think of me as your second mother?'

Rohasena nodded. At that moment Charudatta entered the room along with Maitreya. When he saw Vasantasena's ornaments in his son's clay cart, Charudatta said, 'Oh! Has he taken them from you? Child, give them back at once.'

'No, let him play with them,' begged Vasantasena.

'Very well, I will have them returned to you safely,' said Charudatta.

Rohasena picked up his jewel-laden cart and left the room, followed by his nurse.

After they had left, Vasantasena turned to Charudatta and said, 'I came here to return to you the necklace you sent me. You see, there was no need for it; my original one has already been returned to me.'

Maitreya turned red.

'Impossible! How did you find your necklace?' asked Charudatta in surprise. 'My good lady, I know the nobility of your character. You are only saying this to convince me not to part with this one.'

'Indeed no!' said Vasantasena. 'Sir, please believe me. I cannot tell you how it was returned to me, for it will implicate a person who is not really a thief. His intentions were pure, even if his actions were not. So please take my word for it and let the matter go.'

Turning to Maitreya, she said, 'Sir, kindly take this to the noble Dhuta and beg her forgiveness for the inconvenience I have caused her.'

Maitreya took it, but returned shortly to say, 'The chaste wife of Charudatta says that what her husband has once given away she can no longer consider hers. Hence she asks that you, her younger sister, keep it with her good wishes.'

Taking the necklace, Vasantasena respectfully touched it to her forehead and then put it around her neck. Shortly after that Maitreya went away on some business, leaving Vasantasena and Charudatta alone together.

The night passed happily. When the morning came, the lovers were reluctant to part.

'Spend the day with me,' Charudatta said impulsively. 'I will go ahead to the Pushpakarandaka gardens and prepare a place for us there. Then I will send you the carriage and you may join me.'

She immediately agreed, and Charudatta left. Quickly getting out of bed, Vasantasena was going through the customary rituals of freshening up and getting ready, when she suddenly remembered little Rohasena's words.

'I have chosen as my husband a man who was deprived of his wealth. Hence I too, like Dhuta, shall wear no ornaments.' So, Vasantasena did not put on her jewels and was ready, just as the sound of chariot wheels were heard in the street outside.

The charioteer, meanwhile, thought to himself, 'My master, Samsthanaka, the powerful brother-in-law of king Palaka, asked me to pick him up from the garden of Pushpakarandaka as soon as possible. But now, here is a block in the road! This delay will make him furious, and he is difficult to please as well as vindictive by nature.

Let me go and clear the road myself. It should be safe to leave the chariot standing here, for it is right outside the house of the noble Charudatta.' Sthavaraka dismounted and went off.

A few minutes later, Vasantasena stepped out of Charudatta's house. Mistaking Samsthanaka's chariot for the one Charudatta was supposed to send her, she climbed inside. The road having been cleared, Sthavaraka returned, picked up the reins and set off once again.

The block in the road had been caused by an intensive search for Aryaka, the man who was prophesied to be the next king of Ujjaini. Aryaka had escaped from prison, and now a desperate search was being conducted by the guards of an irate Palaka.

'My master too must be furious at this turn of events. I had better hurry to avoid irritating him further,' thought Sthavaraka, urging the horses to move faster. Before long he reached the garden. Sensing that they had come to a halt, Vasantasena stepped out of the carriage, her heart lifting at the thought of seeing Charudatta again. Instead she found herself face to face with Samsthanaka!

Meanwhile Charudatta's carriage made its way to his house and stopped outside. The charioteer sat where he was, patiently waiting for Vasantasena so that he could take her to meet Charudatta.

But Vasantasena was, of course, miles away. Instead it was Aryaka who came running up, watching anxiously for the king's guards. Just as he was running past the waiting carriage, three guards appeared at the head of the lane.

Aryaka had to act quickly so that he couldn't be seen. He dragged the heavy chains that were still shackled to his legs and slipped into Charudatta's waiting carriage. The guards scanned the lane quickly. Finding it deserted except for a stationary carriage, they went away to look elsewhere. Meanwhile the charioteer thought, 'I felt someone enter the carriage. There was also the sound of anklets. It must have been the lady Vasantasena. Well, I had better be on my way.'

He had, of course, mistaken the sound of Aryaka's chains for Vasantasena's anklets.

When the carriage reached the gardens, Charudatta and Maitreya were there waiting. Charudatta stepped up to help Vasantasena out when he saw a stranger crouched inside.

'Sir, identify yourself!' he commanded.

'I am Aryaka, the unfortunate fellow the king took as prisoner. Are you the Charudatta that all Ujjaini praises?'

'I am Charudatta. I hear you escaped from prison. You must be very careful, for the place is crawling with guards. This time if you are caught there is no telling what they will do to you. You might even be put to death.'

'I am aware of the dangers. Sir, forgive me for imposing on you. I was running away from the king's men when I saw your carriage waiting. I climbed in to hide, and the carriage began to move. I shall get out here and take your leave.'

'You must do no such thing! Tell me, do you have a safe place to go to?'

'I do. I have some loyal friends in a remote country house far from here. If I can make my way there they will gladly hide me.'

'Then use my carriage to get there safely. My charioteer is discreet, he will speak to no one about this. My horses are swift, and should you come upon guards they only need to be told that the vehicle belongs to me and they will let it pass unsearched.'

'Despite the danger I am in, I am glad for this moment that has introduced me to a friend like you. Thank you for your kindness!' said Aryaka with folded hands.

'Please think nothing of it. Go safely and may God be with you!'

After Aryaka had departed, Charudatta turned to Maitreya with a worried frown. 'What could have become of Vasantasena?'

'Perhaps she was left behind at home,' replied Maitreya.

'You are right. We should return there to look for her. She must be growing restless. Let us go.'

Ironically, Vasantasena was in the very same garden at that moment. The horror of her situation hit her the instant she saw Samsthanaka. She gasped and clapped her hand to her mouth.

'What is this?' thought Vita, who was accompanying Samsthanaka. 'The doe has followed the tiger into his den?'

Obtuse as ever, Samsthanaka's face split into a happy grin. 'Vita!' he cried, 'She has come to me. She must have discovered that she loves me after all!'

'A look at her face will reveal that she has only come here by mistake,' said Vita.

'But her eyes have widened in delight at the sight of me! Tears of joy flow from her eyes! She claps her hand to her rose-coloured lips to hide their quivers!'

'Her eyes have widened in shock. Those are tears of horror. She clasps her hand to her mouth to keep herself from screaming out loud.'

'Come to me, my beloved,' said Samsthanaka, approaching Vasantasena. During their previous meeting, Vasantasena had been afraid, for she had still been a courtesan without a protector. But the fact that Charudatta had since claimed her, gave her courage. She stood her ground.

'Sir, Vita,' she said, turning to him. 'I have come only because of a mistaken interchange of carriages. I was supposed to meet Charudatta here. I seek your protection from this evil man.'

Nodding, Vita addressed Samsthanaka firmly, 'You, who are handsome as Kamadeva, wealthy as Kubera, valiant as Indra, I trust you will find little need to force your attentions on a lone and helpless woman. Promise me that you will not approach this lady in any way until I return.'

Not understanding the sarcasm in his words, Samsthanaka immediately puffed out his chest and said, 'What need have

I, a lover among lovers, to approach a woman who doesn't want me?'

'Do I have your word that I will find this woman here when I return?' asked Vita.

'You do,' replied Samsthanaka gravely.

Vita turned to Vasantasena and said, 'My lady, I shall go and find Charudatta and bring him here to you.'

'Please sir, don't go. This man is a liar! I seek your protection!'

'Madam, I assure you, you will be safe. I will be back in no time at all.'

Vita and Sthavaraka left. Some distance away, Vita said to the charioteer, 'My good fellow, go ahead and look for Charudatta. I must double back and make sure the lady is okay. I do not trust Samsthanaka. To be clever and evil is a terrible thing. But to be foolish and evil is a tragedy.'

Hiding himself in the bushes, Vita watched Samsthanaka and Vasantasena. Meanwhile Samsthanaka was thinking, 'That Vita is a smart fellow. I am sure he is watching me discreetly to make sure I am keeping my word. I must behave in such a manner that he is reassured and goes away.'

Smiling politely, Samsthanaka turned to Vasantasena and said, 'My good lady, it is very hot. Won't you rest awhile under the shade of this tree?'

Keeping a wary eye on him, she slowly seated herself. From his hiding place, this exchange looked innocent enough to Vita, and so he went away.

When he was sure the coast was clear, Samsthanaka, without warning, pounced on Vasantasena. She screamed and tried to hit out at him, but he pinned her arms down with one hand, and with the other he took her by the throat.

'Tell me, you daughter-of-a-slave, will you not now accept me?'

Her eyes dilated with terror, Vasantasena shook her head.

'Even if death is the alternative?'

She nodded, desperately trying to draw a breath. At her mute reply, Samsthanaka's large hand tightened further on her throat. Vasantasena struggled and gasped. Her face turned blue, her eyes lost focus. Slowly the frantic thrashing of her limbs stilled. When he released her, she crumpled to the ground, senseless.

'She's dead! Excellent! Now I have shown that lowly courtesan what it is to reject the great Samsthanaka!'

At that moment, Vita and Sthavaraka returned. They hadn't been able to find Charudatta.

'Friend,' said Vita, 'where is the promise you gave me?'

'What promise?' asked Samsthanaka.

'Vasantasena. Safe and well.'

'Oh, that promise! Well, she went away.'

Vita frowned. 'Where?'

'To the South.'

'For what purpose?'

'To meet some relatives of hers.'

'Relatives? Who does she know that lives in the South?'

'Her ancestors, to be precise,' said Samsthanaka, a cruel gleam lighting up his bloodshot eyes.

Vita experienced a sense of growing trepidation. 'You had better speak clearly or I shall forget that you are the king's brother-in-law,' he said in a low, threatening voice.

'You fool, it is the forces of Yama who come from the South and carry off the living to join their ancestors,' said Samsthanaka, pleased with his own wit.

'You killed her!' exclaimed Vita. The anger in his voice made Samsthanaka shrink back in spite of himself.

'There she lies!' cried Sthavaraka, indicating Vasantasena's body under a tree some distance away.

Vita turned on Samsthanaka shouting 'You lowly, filthy son-of-a-dog! May I never set eyes on you again!' Overcome by anger and misery, Vita rushed away. Vasantasena's voice begging, 'Sir, I seek your protection,' ringing in his ears over and over again.

'Sthavaraka, my son, my slave, come, you had better drive me home,' said Samsthanaka to his charioteer.

With trembling hands and a spinning mind, Sthavaraka drove his master back home. He was a good and gentle fellow, and the brutal murder of Vasantasena had shaken him badly. He too would have loved to leave Samsthanaka as Vita had done. But he was a slave, bound to his master for life. The option of walking away was not available to him.

Samsthanaka, meanwhile, was thinking hard. I had better

be on my guard. Soon the news of Vasantasena's murder will be out. I will have to find someone to pin the blame on quickly, before that worthless Vita reports me! What, we have reached? Well, the first thing to do is to imprison the charioteer. The idiot is self-righteous and cowardly, and is bound to blabber something if questions are asked. He stepped out of the carriage and called, 'Sthavaraka, my good slave, come with me.'

The two entered the palace. No sooner did they step inside than Samsthanaka shouted, 'Guards! Chain this fellow and throw him into the topmost room of the tower!'

A terrified Sthavaraka found himself being dragged away.

'I have it!' thought Samsthanaka. 'I will pin this murder on Charudatta. That witch turned me down for him and has paid for it. Now he shall pay for it too! I will go to the courthouse this very instant and initiate a trial against him.'

In the meanwhile, Charudatta and Maitreya had reached home and found Vasantasena gone.

'Perhaps she has returned to her own house,' suggested Maitreya.

'You are right, that is the only explanation. Friend, please take this bundle of jewels to her and tell her that I shall come to see her in the evening.'

'What jewels are these?' asked Maitreya.

'The ones she had filled Rohasena's clay cart with.'

'Very well, I shall go right away.'

Maitreya left and Charudatta was just washing the dust of the journey from his feet when a clerk from the courthouse appeared at his door.

'Sir,' said the clerk respectfully, "You have been summoned to the court.'

'For what purpose?' asked Charudatta, puzzled.

The clerk dropped his eyes in discomfort. 'There has been a murder.'

'My left eye throbs,' thought Charudatta with a sense of foreboding. 'No good will come of this day.' Without a word he left the house and made his way to the courthouse.

When he entered the courtroom, he found the judge in his usual place looking grave. He stood up when Charudatta entered, because such was the respect the noble Charudatta commanded in Ujjaini.

'Fool,' yelled a voice from the front of the room, 'do you stand up for a man who is wanted for murder?'

Turning his head, Charudatta saw it was Samsthanaka who had spoken.

'Be quiet!' said the judge. 'There is no doubt in anybody's mind that Charudatta is incapable of murder, that too the murder of a woman.' (Charudatta gave a start.) 'We have brought him here to prove his innocence, not his guilt!'

'Very well then. Begin,' said Samsthanaka.

'Sir,' said the judge respectfully, turning to Charudatta, 'Do you know a lady by the name of Vasantasena?'

'I do,' replied Charudatta, beginning to grow agitated.

'But what of her? And who is this woman who has been murdered?'

'Commendable acting!' applauded Samsthanaka with a derisive laugh.

'Silence!' cried the judge. 'Sir, Charudatta, were you supposed to meet this woman today?'

'Yes, in the Pushpakarandaka gardens. But she did not come although I waited long for her.'

'You mean in the Pushpakarandaka gardens where you killed her,' shouted Samsthanaka.

'No! What is this man saying?' cried Charudatta. 'Killed? Is Vasantasena dead then?'

'Compose yourself, sir,' said the judge gently.

'I cannot, unless you tell me what has become of the lady!'

'She was found murdered in the Pushpakarandaka gardens.'

'No!' cried Charudatta, fainting.

'Let us get past the drama, gentlemen,' said Samsthanaka. 'Call in Charudatta's servant and Vasantasena's maid. They will confirm that she left Charudatta's home in his carriage and headed out to the gardens to meet him.'

The maid and the servant were summoned, and both of them fearfully testified that this was true. At this the judges began to look a little uncomfortable. Charudatta, who had revived, now sat still and white-faced, like a man who was suffering from some deadly internal wound.

'Now call in Vasantasena's mother,' said Samsthanaka.

When the old lady arrived in court, she saw Charudatta and thought, 'My daughter has chosen well. She could find no better man to give her youth away to.'

As yet unaware of her daughter's death she testified proudly, 'Yes, this is the man my daughter loves. In fact she spent all of last night with him and still has not returned home.'

By now the judges were looking grave. At that very moment, Maitreya came rushing into the courtroom, the bundle of jewels still clutched in his hands.

'Charudatta!' he cried, 'I heard in the streets that you were being tried for the murder of Vasantasena. I had to come directly here and see what was going on! Oh how can they suspect you, the best of men?'

'What is that in your hands, you rogue?' asked Samsthanaka. He made a grab at the bundle and it fell to the floor and split open. The jewels scattered everywhere.

'Whose ornaments are these?' demanded Samsthanaka.

'They are Vasantasena's!' cried the weeping mother.

'There you have it!' exclaimed Samsthanaka. 'Now the truth is evident. Here you have the murderer.' He pointed accusingly at Charudatta, 'And there is the motive for the murder!' He drew everyone's attention to the ornaments on the floor.

'Sir, everything seems to be working against you. Please tell us, did you murder the lady Vasantasena?' asked the judge.

Charudatta sat there, his face turned to stone. The only

thought on his mind was, I have lost my reputation and my beloved.

'Sir,' said the Judge insistently, 'Please answer us. Did you murder Vasantasena?'

Charudatta turned his dazed eyes upon the judge thinking, with my reputation and Vasantasena gone, death will be a boon. Besides what is the use of speaking? Nobody will take the word of a poor man. So he remained silent.

With a heavy sigh of resignation, the judge spoke. 'This court finds Charudatta guilty of the murder of the courtesan Vasantasena. It is not for us to put a Brahmin to death. Hence let the king decide his punishment.'

A messenger was sent to the king. Within minutes he returned with a verdict. Charudatta was to be executed!

Samsthanaka was jubilant. But Vasantasena's mother burst into renewed tears, and Maitreya was plunged in despair. The judges looked grave and troubled, while the common people of Ujjaini were outraged. Hundreds flocked to the courthouse—people who had benefited from Charudatta's generosity, well-wishers, friends—to beg for Charudatta's life. But the king's verdict was irrevocable.

Only one man remained stoic, and that was Charudatta himself. When the guards came for him, he made no protest, submitting quietly to being chained and taken away. He was followed by the citizens of Ujjaini.

When the procession reached the execution ground, two

Chandalas stepped forward and took charge of Charudatta. Bowing to him they said sadly, 'This is the gloomiest day of our lives. It is one thing to execute a sinner. But to put to death a noble man ... Sir, forgive us for what we are about to do.'

'Have no regrets,' said Charudatta. 'You are only doing your duty. There is no right or wrong attached to that.'

'Good people of Ujjaini,' cried one of the Chandalas, 'Make way! Why do you wait here? Don't you know that to witness the execution of a virtuous man can bring great misfortune? Make way!'

Still the people waited, reluctant to leave the benefactor they all loved alone in his death.

Turning to the weeping Maitreya, Charudatta said, 'You stood by me when my good fortune deserted me. Hence I ask you for one last favour. Look after Rohasena and my beloved Dhuta.'

'O my friend, do not ask me this one thing!' begged Maitreya brokenly. 'For it is a promise I cannot fulfil.'

'Do not let me down, Maitreya!' said Charudatta.

'I cannot help it. For I will not be able to continue in this world without you. After your death, I too shall give up my life.'

'Do not speak that way. You are young and will live a long and happy life.'

'Every minute beyond your death will be a curse to me!'

'Maitreya, a son is the living continuation of one's

existence on this earth. Hence give my Rohasena all the love that you have reserved for me,' said Charudatta.

One Chandala whispered to the other, 'Let us delay this execution for as long as possible. Who knows, perhaps from somewhere someone might appear to clear this man of his guilt.'

'You are right,' replied the other. 'Lives like this deserve to be saved.'

Suddenly there was a commotion on the outer periphery of the crowd. Everybody turned to look, and they saw Sthavaraka, the charioteer of Samsthanaka, running awkwardly towards them, his limbs still weighed down by iron chains.

Samsthanaka, who was in the crowd, gave a start. 'I knew I should have put that idiot to death! However did he manage to break free from that tower?'

Stepping forward he shouted, 'What are you doing here?'

'Stop the execution!' cried Sthavaraka. 'For I am witness to Samsthanaka's confession of having killed Vasantasena with his own hands! It was not Charudatta who killed the lady. In fact he was nowhere near the scene of the crime. Samsthanaka is the culprit!'

The crowd turned on Samsthanaka with an angry hiss.

'He lies!' cried Samsthanaka. 'He is my slave, and I recently had him flogged and imprisoned for stealing some gold ornaments!' Then in a whisper Samsthanaka said to the charioteer, 'Son, my slave, take this gold bracelet and hold your peace! This is not all, I will reward you well when we return home.'

'What?' asked the latter, as the bracelet was thrust forcibly into his hand, 'Are you bribing me?'

Samsthanaka acted quickly. He snatched back the bracelet in full view of the people saying, 'Look, see, here is the gold this thief stole from me, for which I had him punished. Otherwise where would a slave like him come in possession of something so fine?'

'He is right,' said the crowd. 'What won't a slave say when he is angry with his master?'

In despair, Sthavaraka turned to Charudatta. 'Sir, forgive me. I did my best to clear your name, but nobody takes the word of a poor man!'

'Thank you for your efforts. I know you have done this at great personal risk,' replied Charudatta.

At that moment, a woman was stirring in the Pushpakarandaka gardens. It was Vasantasena! She was not dead after all. She had only lost consciousness for some time. As she came to, a monk passed that way. It was Samvahaka, the gambler whom Vasantasena had helped. True to his word, he had joined the Buddhist order and was now walking through the gardens, when Vasantasena's groans caught his ears.

'Who is that?' he thought, hurrying over to her side. 'Why, it is the noble lady Vasantasena to whom I owe my life! Madam, take my hand and rise. Here, you may rest your weight on me.'

He led her to a pond where he gave her water to drink. Refreshed, Vasantasena said, 'Sir, be so kind as to accompany me to the house of Charudatta.'

Happy to do anything he could for her, Samvahaka slowly led her out of the gardens. As they entered the main streets of Ujjaini, they found the place deserted.

'Something seems to be wrong,' said Samvahaka with a worried frown. 'Brother,' he hailed a lone passerby, 'what is going on here?'

'Holy one, they are putting the good Charudatta to death.'

Vasantasena swayed and Samvahaka quickly steadied her. 'For what crime?' he asked.

'For the murder of the courtesan Vasantasena. They might be executing him even as we speak.'

Without a word Vasantasena turned and broke into a run towards the execution grounds. She did not notice the heat of the sun or her own exhaustion. She only ran as if her life depended on it.

At the execution grounds the Chandalas prepared Charudatta, tying his hands and legs and laying him down. 'Sir, have no fear,' they said to him. 'We are skilled at our job and will execute you quickly and painlessly.'

'Vasantasena, my beloved! Wherever you are, may you prove my innocence and restore my reputation after I am gone,' prayed Charudatta silently, then closed his eyes in preparation for death.

Just as one of the Chandalas raised his axe, a woman's

voice was heard crying, 'Stop! Nobody is to execute this man, for Vasantasena is very much alive!'

A shocked murmur went through the crowd.

'Who is that?'

'It is Vasantasena herself! Alive!'

'Praise be to God! Charudatta is saved!' cried the people as one.

Charudatta raised his head and saw her. 'My beloved! You came just as my heart called out to you!'

Throwing her body across his protectively, Vasantasena shouted at the stunned Chandalas, 'Stop! Lower the axe! And if you must raise it again, let it be to cut off the head of the evil Samsthanaka, who is the one who really tried to kill me!'

The crowd turned angrily to where Samsthanaka had been standing, and found him gone.

'There he goes, the coward! Catch him! Put him to death!'

They dragged him back, kicking and struggling, and hurled him at Charudatta's feet. 'He is yours. Punish him as you see fit!'

'Will my verdict be accepted?' asked Charudatta.

'Without question.'

'Then release this man and let him go. The only way to conquer hate is to overwhelm it with love.'

Reluctantly the crowd did as Charudatta asked, and the wretched Samsthanaka turned tail and ran. He was never seen or heard of again.

Just then a messenger came running up. It was

Sarvilaka!

'People,' he cried, 'I bring you good news! Aryaka along with his band of loyal followers has overthrown Palaka and declared himself king of Ujjaini!'

A jubilant cry rose from the crowd, and the skies rang with it.

'The instant he came to the throne, Aryaka bestowed the kingdom of Kusavati on Charudatta,' continued Sarvilaka, raising his voice to be heard above the cheering. 'He has also conferred upon lady Vasantasena the title of Second Wife to Charudatta!'

The crowds cheered louder still. Vasantasena and Charudatta looked at each other, tears of joy filling their eyes. And so Charudatta, restored to his former wealth and position, took his new bride home, where the good Dhuta received her like a sister.

Uttararamacharita

Bhavabhuti

It is believed that the Ramayana was composed by the great sage Valmiki sometime around the second century BC. Since it is impossible to improve on perfection, Bhavabhuti, with no sense of competition, simply wrote a version of his own.

The Uttararamacharita is a Sanskrit play based on the final kanda (part) of the original epic. It begins with the coronation of Rama after his return to Ayodhya from the forest. The play culminates in an entirely novel way. Not only is the ending different from what the audience expects, but Bhavabhuti has also devised an ingenious plot in which gods and humans and the various elements of nature conspire elaborately to make it happen. The story ends with a play-within-the-play, until what is enacted on stage becomes a reality. The audience (the citizens of Ayodhya, Rama and other members of the royal family) all find themselves unwittingly becoming principal characters in the story that is being staged before them.

Bhavabhuti is believed to be a contemporary of Kalidasa. He is named among the foremost dramatists and poets of all time. Bhavabhuti's mastery over Vedic lore and his familiarity with the literature of the Upanishads *are evident in his writing.* Mahaviracharita, Malati-Madhava *and* Uttararamacharita *make up the body of his literary works.*

The Last Trial of Sita

The war is over. Ravana of Lanka is dead. Sita, having proved her chastity with the test of fire and emerged from the flames unharmed, is reunited with Rama.

The story opens in Ayodhya, the capital of the Raghu Dynasty. Rama has recently been reinstated to the throne with great joy and celebration. Brahmins and sages, monkeys and asuras travelled from hundreds of yojanas away to share in the festivities. They have now departed. The queen mother Kaushalya, with the virtuous Arundhati and sage Vashishta, has gone to the hermitage of her son-in-law to attend a yagna.

The story that follows is one of honour and dharma; of sacrifice made at a terrible price ...

But let's not get ahead of the tale. The sad times are still a little way off. Today there is only joy in the heart of Ayodhya's king. Reunited with his beloved wife, Rama rules his people justly and wisely, believing them to be as happy as he himself is.

After a long day at court Rama enters his chambers to find Sita, who is expecting their baby soon, tired and resting. Just as he sits down beside her, a messenger of sage Vashishta asks to meet him.

Rising quickly, the king and queen go out to receive him.

'Revered Sir, do sit down. Are my elders all well?' asks Rama.

'They are, Your Majesty. I bring to you a message from sage Vashishta. But first, a message from Mother Kaushalya. She instructs that even the smallest of the Queen's pregnancy cravings must be met instantly, in much the same manner that she herself would have ensured had she been here.'

With a gentle smile of amusement, Rama nods his agreement.

'And now for the holy one's message ...'

Rama rises to receive the word of his guru with folded hands.

'"You (His Majesty) are young, and have only just ascended the throne. Let your every action be directed towards the happiness of your people. The glory from that is, and always has been, the highest treasure of the Raghu Dynasty." These, Your Majesty, were his very words,' says the messenger.

'I receive them as my greatest dharma. Friendship, personal happiness, even my beloved Sita I shall sacrifice without regret if it is in the interest of my people,' replies Rama with sincerity.

Just then Lakshmana joins them. 'Your Majesty, the paintings we had commissioned have arrived.'

'What is this?' asks Sita with a puzzled smile.

'Paintings depicting the life of the king,' replies Lakshmana.

'Come Sita, come Lakshmana, let us go and see them,' says Rama, after the messenger has left.

The three of them walk among the paintings, reliving moments in their lives both happy and sad. The artist had breathed life and sensibility into the canvas with skill and grace.

They look upon their younger selves—Rama and Lakshmana together with Bharata and Shatruguna—in their boyhood days of study, living in the home of their teacher; their return home; their wedding day. Young Rama holding the hand of twelve-year-old Sita, tender and beautiful. Lakshmana notices himself and Urmila, the younger sister of Sita, waiting their turn to be called for their own wedding ceremony.

'Oh, what are these?' asks Sita, breaking into Lakshmana's thoughts.

'They are the mysterious Jrimbhaka missiles that were revealed to Vashishta, and were in turn presented to my brother by the royal sage,' replies Lakshmana.

'Offer your homage to them, Sita,' says Rama, coming up to stand behind her. 'The Creator Brahma himself, having practised penance for over a thousand years, conceived those missiles from his own spiritual energies.'

Sita bows before the painting reverentially.

'As of this moment, they will reveal their secrets to the child you are carrying, just as they have revealed them to me,' utters Rama.

They move on, reliving the happy days after their marriage, when they had returned to Ayodhya from Mithila. 'Our beloved father was still alive then. And how our mothers took care of us! Oh what wonderful days those were!'

'And who is this?' asks Sita curiously, stopping before the figure of a twisted old hag.

'Manthara,' and Lakshmana shoots an uncertain glance at her face.

'Look here my dear!' interrupts Rama quickly. 'Look at how beautifully the artist has captured you in this painting!'

Lakshmana realises that Rama is deliberately drawing Sita's attention away from the illustration of Kaikeyi demanding his exile to the forest.

They move on to the scenes describing their happy years in the lush forests of Dandaka. 'Here we are, the three of us, you, me and our faithful Lakshmana,' says Rama, turning affectionate eyes on his brother.

'My Lord, this painting makes me long to return to Dandaka. How I wish to go and spend a few hours there, sipping from the cool streams, playing among the deer and the peacocks!' sighs Sita.

'Then you shall go. Mother Kaushalya instructed that you must be given everything your heart wishes.' Turning to

Lakshmana, Rama says, 'Brother, prepare a chariot for the queen, one that does not jolt too much.'

Lakshmana hurries away to do his brother's bidding.

'Won't you go with me?' asks Sita, looking up at her husband.

'Need you even ask, my love?' replies Rama, smiling down at her. 'But come, you must rest first.'

Within minutes Sita falls deeply asleep, a soft smile of happiness playing about her lips. Rama gazes down at her, remembering how she had been snatched from him so abruptly and cruelly by Ravana. Recalling the emptiness and despair of those months of separation, a shudder passes through him. Sita, unaware of her husband's turmoiled thoughts, sleeps on peacefully.

'I mustn't think of those days,' Rama tells himself sternly. 'She is here in my arms, carrying my child in her womb. We will never be apart again.' This thought comforts him and he relaxes once more.

A sound at the door draws him out of his reverie.

'Who is it?'

'It is I, Durmukha, Your Majesty.'

'Durmukha!' thinks Rama to himself. 'My personal attendant, whom I had commissioned to secretly find out the thoughts of my people!' Gently easing his arm from under Sita's head and replacing it with a pillow, he rises to his feet saying with a smile of welcome, 'Enter, friend! What news?'

'Oh, how can I communicate to my gentle king the terrible thoughts that the subjects he loves so well have against him?' thinks Durmukha frantically. 'I would rather die than repeat the scandalous words that come from their foul and suspicious minds! Yet, I should not fool him into thinking that all is well.'

'What is it, Durmukha? You look troubled.'

'My lord, where are you?' mumbles Sita in her sleep, restlessly tossing her head.

Rama turns to look at her. 'The sight of the painting, the scenes of her abduction and long separation from me have disturbed her mind like they disturbed mine.' He places a loving hand on her forehead, and Sita, soothed, falls back into deep slumber.

Durmukha is touched at this demonstration of love and quickly turns away. But Rama's insistent hand on his shoulder forces him to meet the king's eyes again.

'I know there is bad news,' says Rama quietly. 'Durmukha, you must tell me the truth.'

'Then listen to it, my lord, and forgive me for being the bearer of such news.' Leaning close to the king, Durmukha whispers a few words into his ear.

Rama reels away, as if struck by a heavy hand. 'How demeaning are these suspicions that cling to a woman who has lived in the home of another man! My pure and innocent Queen, who passed those months in Ravana's kingdom with her thoughts fixed on me alone, is not to be left in peace.

She was so pure that even the fire could not bear to touch her, and yet, now this ...'

He paces up and down restlessly, his mind whirling, while Durmukha looks on miserably.

'What am I to do? And yet, what else is there to be done? My people come first. Father upheld his promise, sacrificing me for his honour even though it cost him his life. In this way he fulfilled his duty as a king. This has always been the tradition of the Raghus. So what right do I have to ruin the spotless reputation of my forefathers by a scandal of this nature? Just today my Guru Vashishta sent me a message saying, 'Let your every action be directed towards the happiness of your people.' What choice do I have? There is only one course of action left for me!'

Turning sadly to his sleeping wife, Rama mutters brokenly, 'My gentle and virtuous wife, how is it that you are to be wronged in this way again and again?' He drops to his knees and weeps into his hands.

Durmukha is almost numb with misery at the sight of his king's distress.

Suddenly Rama raises his head. The burning determination in his eyes is frightening, and Durmukha unwittingly takes a step back.

'Durmukha, tell Prince Lakshmana to take the Queen to the Dandaka forest as planned. He is to leave her there and return home alone.'

'No!' cries Durmukha, the impact of Rama's words hitting him. 'I beg of you, don't do this. She is pregnant. My lord, she will not survive! Of what importance are slanderous words coming from filthy minds? Why must the innocent Queen suffer for it?'

'I know my Queen is pure. But as long as the people do not believe it, what example may we hope to set them, we, who are father and mother to them? What morality, what law and order can I uphold in this kingdom when the minds of my people are full of doubt? No, regardless of what it costs me, Sita must go.'

And so, Sita goes. Anticipating a pleasant afternoon in the shady valleys of the Dandaka forest with Rama, she is instead informed that the king is unexpectedly caught up in matters of state. Innocent of what is in store for her, she leaves home expecting to return in a few hours. Instead, she finds herself abandoned.

The hour of childbirth arrives. Alone, helpless, tortured by the pain tearing at her insides, Sita is sure that she is going to die. But fate has other plans. She brings forth, instead, twin boys, brilliant as the sun.

***

Twelve years have passed. Here we are now, once more in the forests of Dandaka. But what is going on? It appears that the forest deity Vasanti is engaged in conversation with ...

'Atreyi!'

'I have come from the ashram of Valmiki.'

'Revered lady, I bow to you. What brings you here?' asks Vasanti.

'My quest for knowledge of the Vedas,' replies the female ascetic.

'Then surely you must go back home! For who better to teach you than Sage Valmiki himself?' exclaims Vasanti.

'It is true that he is master of the Vedas. But a problem has come up.'

'Of what kind?'

'Twelve years ago a goddess presented the great sage with twin boys, Lava and Khusha. She did not reveal the names of the children's parents to anyone except the sage.'

'And?'

Dropping her voice, Atreyi continues, 'These boys have a certain power ...'

Interestedly, Vasanti leans closer.

'They possess the knowledge of the mystical Jrimbhaka missiles from birth itself.'

'How strange! For I know that apart from Lord Brahma and Sage Valmiki, the only other mortal who knows those spells is King Rama.'

'True,' replies Atreyi, 'which is what makes these two boys so marvellous. The holy Valmiki himself raised them from infancy. Now he instructs them in the principles of Vedanta along with the rest of us. But these young children have mastered them so rapidly that the rest of us are left behind. There is another obstacle to my learning. Sage Valmiki has been commissioned by Lord Brahma to write the story of Rama. So, for some years now the sage has been busy with the task of recording the king's exemplary life on parchment. It is to be called the *Ramayana*.'

'A worthy task indeed!' exclaims Vasanti happily. 'So the holy one has been too busy to instruct you further?'

'That's why I have come here in search of another teacher. Friend, tell me where I might find Sage Agastya?'

'His hermitage is a little away from here. Enter the Panchvati and follow the banks of the Godavari.'

'What? Is this the Dandaka forest then?' cries Atreyi. 'Then you must be Vasanti, the deity of this forest!'

'That is correct,' replies Vasanti.

'I cannot help but think of you, daughter Sita! I stand before your friend who loved you so dearly while you lived here!' mutters Atreyi with tears in her eyes.

'Holy one, is all not well with Sita then?'

Leaning forward, Atreyi sadly spills out the story of Sita's misfortune in Vasanti's unhappy ear.

'How can this be? How could Vashishta and Arundhati and Mother Kaushalya permit this?' cries Vasanti.

'They were not present when it happened. And they are so disturbed by it that, even after the twelve-year-long sacrifice at their son-in-law's home has concluded, they

have refused to return to Ayodhya. At this moment that are on their way to the hermitage of Valmiki to take up residence there.'

'And King Rama? How is he engaged now?'

'In the great horse sacrifice, the Ashwamedha yagna.'

'Without a consort? That is impossible. No yagna can be performed by a man alone. That means he must have married again. O shame on him!' says Vasanti angrily.

'Indeed no!' Atreyi hastily adds. 'He is still true to Sita. He places beside him a golden image of her when he sits down at the yagna.'

'How strange,' says Vasanti, softening. 'Harder even than stone, yet softer than a flower are the hearts of righteous men. Who can truly understand them?'

'The sacrificial horse has been consecrated and let loose. Its guardian is Prince Chandraketu, son of Lakshmana, initiated into the use of the heavenly weapons. He is accompanied by all the four divisions of Rama's mighty army.'

Atreyi looks up at the sky. 'Friend,' she says, 'give me leave. It is late and I must be on my way.'

'Goodbye, and go in peace.'

Back in Ayodhya, a Brahmin has just laid down the body of his dead son at Rama's feet crying, 'Look, O king! All is not well in your kingdom!'

Rama leaps to his feet and looks at the dead youth with despair.

'This must be a result of something I have done,' he mutters. 'Only the misconduct of the king can bring premature death to his subjects.'

'Not true, O king!' a celestial voice rings out. 'A shudra, Sambuka by name, has been practising religious austerities. Only Brahmins have the right to do that. His actions are causing terrible things to happen on earth. You must do your duty, King Rama. Cut off Sambuka's head and restore this Brahmin boy to life.'

Immediately Rama gathers up his weapons, mounts his chariot and rides out. He rides until he finds the shudra in the middle of a dense forest, deep in austerities. He raises his sword over Sambuka's head when suddenly he is uncertain about what he is about to do.

'Why this hesitation? You, who could abandon innocent Sita in the wilderness while she was carrying your child? Surely, great Rama, after something like that this should be easy!' he thinks in self-loathing. In one swift blow he separates the man's head from his body.

Within seconds a spirit appears before his glazed eyes.

'Greetings, O king.'

'Are you Sambuka?' asks Rama quietly.

'I am. Even death at your hands can bring salvation. I bow to you.'

'May you experience heaven and all its joys,' Rama blesses him.

'I am on my way there now, Lord. I will only stop to pay homage to Sage Agastya before I depart.'

After Sambuka leaves, Rama slowly gets to his feet and looks around. He realises that he is in the Dandaka forest. 'The place where I spent so many months with my Sita! Here we sat and ... and there did I hold her in my arms.'

Suddenly there is the sound of footsteps, and Rama turns around to find that Sambuka has returned.

'Lord, I come with a message from Sage Agastya. He and his wife Lopamudra ask that you honour them with a visit before you return to Ayodhya.'

Sambuka departs for heaven, and Rama immediately turns his chariot in the direction of Sage Agastya's hermitage.

At the hermitage, Lopamudra looks upon the emaciated form of Rama with concern. Soon after he sets out for Dandaka again, she sends for Murala, one of the young girls of the hermitage. 'How the grief of parting from Sita has weakened him! I am frightened by his condition. While he was in the kingdom, his kingly duties kept him occupied. But here, memories of his happy days with Sita are bound to upset him. Murala, send word to River Godavari to watch over him until he has left the forest safely.'

'Mother, let me set your mind at rest. My friend told me that on Goddess Ganga's instruction, Tamasa has brought Sita under some pretext to Dandaka for the very purpose of soothing Rama, should his distress be too great.'

'O clever Ganga! Who better to console the king than his Sita? Child, you have made me happy with this bit of news!' says Lopamudra happily.

'Mother, can you imagine Sita's joy at the first sight of her husband after twelve long years?' asks Murala.

Here is the forest and there is Sita, beautiful as ever. With her is Tamasa. The two women turn their heads at the sound of chariot wheels. It seems Rama too has arrived! Unaware that his beloved is close by, Rama alights and looks around. Slowly he approaches a kadamba tree growing nearby, touching its branches in wonder. 'This tree! It is the one from which I gathered flowers for my Sita's hair.'

From the thicket beyond Sita gives a start. 'I hear my husband's voice! Is it true? Is he really here, or is this like the thousand other times when I heard his voice and looked for him, only to find I had imagined it?'

'No child, it is King Rama,' replies Tamasa. 'He was here to behead the shudra Sambuka.'

'Then he isn't neglecting his kingly duties. I'm glad to know that,' says Sita, unconsciously moving towards the sound of Rama's voice. 'There he is! I never thought I would see him again. I am blessed!'

Sita, hidden away among the trees, stands transfixed, her gaze clinging to Rama, unable to tear herself away. But as she drinks in the sight of him, her joy turns to sorrow.

'Look at him. He is so weakened and emaciated! He too has suffered as I have. I can bear all my sufferings, but not his. Oh mother, not his!' she weeps.

'Be strong, child,' says Tamasa, laying a soothing hand on Sita's arm.

Meanwhile Rama wanders here and there restlessly. 'That stone slab! We lay there, my Sita and I, hidden away from the world in our most intimate moments.'

Hearing his words, Sita's heart contracts with pain. She reaches out a hand to him, as if to bridge the distance separating them.

Suddenly there is a soft sound in the clearing beyond and Rama turns quickly. 'That deer! Oh, he is the little creature my Sita adopted and raised as her own child!'

The deer recognises Rama and gambols up to him, resting its head lovingly on his thigh, looking up at him with soft, intelligent eyes. Caressing its head Rama says, 'Child, you are asking me for your mother. But I do not know where she is. I do not know, for I, wretch that I am, sent her away. Perhaps she is dead ...' The tears in Rama's eyes blind him and he falls, fainting.

'Oh!' cries Sita miserably. 'I'm here, Lord, I'm here!'

'Go child, revive your husband with the touch of your hand,' says Tamasa.

'But how can I approach him? He had his own reasons for separating me from himself. How can I stand before him now? Surely it will increase his unhappiness if I do so?'

'The goddess Ganga has made you invisible. Even if you approach him he will not be able to see you.'

Sita walks up to Rama's unconscious form and places her hands gently and lovingly on his forehead and over his heart. The king's eyes open and he sits up, looking around quickly. 'My darling, where are you? I know your touch, I smell your fragrance on the breeze. I beg you, show yourself to me!'

But Sita tearfully backs away.

'Come,' says Tamasa, gently but insistently. 'Let us join Ganga now at Valmiki's hermitage. They say there is a great play to be staged there. Perhaps being a part of the festivities will cheer you up.'

Tamasa steers a weeping Sita away from the forest.

At Valmiki's hermitage, Sita's father, king Janaka of Mithila, accompanied by Kaushalya and Arundhati, is strolling among the gardens.

'Queen Kaushalya was once radiant and glowing like the goddess of Wealth. Now I can barely recognise her, so pale and grief-worn has she become,' thinks Janaka sadly to himself. 'Has the loss of Sita done this to her? Words of bitterness and anger died on my lips the moment I laid eyes on her. For how could I add to her grief by accusations?'

And Kaushalya, as she walks beside Janaka, thinks, 'I suffer so much from Sita's absence. How grieved and angry he, her father, must be. Yet he hid his pain and enquired after Rama with words that only a father would use while speaking of his own son. Indeed, I am shamed more deeply by his kindness.'

Suddenly there is a noise and the sound of young voices. They turn around and see a young boy of twelve, bright eyed, blue-skinned, with soft curls blowing about his face. Both Kaushalya and Janaka are struck by how familiar he looks.

'O King, doesn't this child resemble our daughter Sita, with his curly locks and moon-like face?' asks Kaushalya.

'Yes, and his skin is blue like Rama's. His noble bearing, his air of command along with an underlying gentleness, all bring to mind our son.'

'Little one,' calls out Kaushalya, 'come to me.'

The boy approaches, bowing respectfully to them.

'Dear child, who are your parents?' asks Janaka.

'Revered one, I do not know. I belong to Sage Valmiki, who raised me from infancy. My name is Lava.'

A commotion draws everybody's attention to the forest a little distance away. A messenger comes running up and bows to Kaushalya. 'Your Highness, Prince Chandraketu, the guardian of the sacrificial horse, has arrived!'

Kaushalya's face lights up.

'May I ask who this Chandraketu is?' says Lava, turning to King Janaka.

'Have you heard of Rama and Lakshmana of Ayodhya?' asks the king.

'Of course! Who hasn't? They are the heroes of the *Ramayana*!' replies Lava.

'Chandraketu is the son of Lakshmana.'

'Then he was born of Urmila and is the grandson of the royal sage Janaka, king of Mithila!' cries Lava enthusiastically.

'That is correct,' replies Janaka with a smile in his eyes, while Kaushalya and Arundhati laugh silently at the endearing child.

'Tell us, since you seem so well acquainted with the story, what are the names of the other grandchildren of King Dasharatha?' asks Arundhati teasingly.

'I do not know,' replies the boy earnestly, 'for Sage Valmiki, who is writing the *Ramayana*, has not revealed that portion of the text to anyone. He has, instead, composed it as a separate piece of work, and sent it on to the venerable sage Bharata.'

'For what purpose?'

'To be enacted as a play by the heavenly nymphs before the world. He is so happy with the manuscript that the revered Valmiki has sent my brother Kusha, bow in hand, to safeguard it along the way.'

'Have you a brother too then?' asks Kaushalya.

'Yes, a twin who is elder by order of birth.'

'Child, tell me what kind of ending the story of Valmiki's *Ramayana* has?' asks Janaka.

'The holy one stopped at the point where Lakshmana left the pregnant Queen Sita in the forest and returned home alone.'

Janaka turns away as if the child's words are too much for him to bear, while Kaushalya, suddenly overcome, breaks down and weeps.

Lava gazes at them in puzzlement. But the sudden entry of his schoolmates distracts him.

'Lava! There is a horse wandering in these parts. Come, we must go look at it for we have never seen one before!'

Bowing before them, Lava says charmingly, 'Give me leave, I am being dragged away against my will.'

'Go with our blessings, dear child,' says Arundhati.

'What is this bond I feel with that boy? It is as if I cannot live a moment longer if I am parted from him,' says Kaushalya, while Janaka looks after the departing child with longing.

Meanwhile Lava's friends go up to the soldiers accompanying the horse. 'Sires, why does this horse roam about guarded?'

'Don't you know? It is a sacrificial horse,' replies Lava before the soldiers can speak. 'It is the ultimate test of the supreme power of one great king over all the others.'

'Your friend is right,' says a soldier. Adding proudly, 'And this horse—the banner it carries—belongs to the conqueror of the seven worlds, the destroyer of the race of Ravana!'

'What arrogance!' cries Lava. 'Are there no other worthy Kshatriyas left in this world that you should speak this way? Here, I carry off this banner from under your nose!' Smartly lifting the banner, the boy walks away.

'Child,' cries the soldier in alarm, 'Come back! What you are doing is foolishness! The challenger of King Rama's power will face the wrath of Prince Chandraketu and his entire army.'

But Lava walks on without a backward glance, followed by his friends.

Before long there is chaos in the ranks of Rama's army. It starts with the rumour that the banner has been abducted. Then word spreads that a twelve-year-old is the culprit.

'Huh!' shrugs a soldier, turning over and preparing to go back to sleep. 'The poor child must have done it as a joke.'

'You're right. Someone go tell his parents and they will scold him and return the banner,' agrees another.

'No! No! You don't understand!' cries the bearer of the news. 'This boy openly challenged the power of our king!'

As the word spreads it becomes apparent that the soldiers will have to take up arms. Most of them do so laughingly, shaking their heads at the absurdity of engaging a mere child in armed combat.

But soon they stop laughing. For, in almost no time at all, Lava raises his bow and disarms the whole of Rama's army single-handedly!

When the news reaches Chandraketu, he rushes to the site of battle. In spite of himself he is thoroughly impressed.

'Wonderful! Look at the way this little child wields his bow! It is obvious our men stand no chance against him.' Raising his voice Chandraketu calls out, 'Little man, what have you to do with these soldiers? Here is Chandraketu standing before you. Pit your bow against mine. Let valour be faced with valour and then the outcome will be fair.'

Taking advantage of his momentary distraction, the fleeing soldiers quickly return to surround Lava. Seeing this Lava is angered.

'What cowards they are!' he cries, falling on them with lightning speed and sending them scurrying once again.

Chandraketu's heart fills with inexplicable pride and affection for this brave child.

'I admire you for your absolute courage and skill!' he cries. 'Although I will fight you, you are my friend. Therefore, whatever belongs to me belongs to you also, even victory!' Saying this, Chandraketu evokes a heavenly missile and fires it at Lava. Lava quickly counters it with a timely arrow. Chandraketu evokes another and once again Lava blocks it. Then Lava evokes a missile of his own.

Soon the air is rent with brilliant lights and raging fires, icy winds and ear-splitting shrieks. The world trembles and even the gods from their heavens come to witness the heroic battle between the two princes of the solar race.

Then Lava calls forth the Jrimbhaka missile. At that very moment, Rama, who is returning home from Dandaka, sees the young boy discharging the weapon, and is overcome by astonishment and curiosity. He quickly rides up to the site of the battle.

Chandraketu immediately lowers his bow and prostrates himself before the feet of his uncle. Awed by the magnetism of Rama's mere presence, Lava's fervour cools and he stands by quietly while Rama embraces Chandraketu warmly.

'Father,' says Chandraketu, 'This is Lava, a boy of tremendous courage and skill. Since he is my friend I hope you will look upon him with as much affection as you look upon me.'

Rama marks Lava closely. 'Son, come to me,' he says, extending a hand to Lava.

'How great this man is. How serene and wise are his eyes. Under his gaze all my anger and haughty pride seem to melt away,' thinks Lava as he bows before Rama.

As he holds the child, Rama's heart lifts with joy. 'For the first time since the day I abandoned Sita in the forest, the void in my soul seems to be filled. How is it that this child's presence soothes my grief of twelve long years?' he wonders.

'Chandraketu, who is this?' asks Lava when he steps away.

'My father.'

'Then he is the same to me by the laws of relationship, for you have called me your friend. But there are four heroes in the *Ramayana*. Which of them is he?' asks Lava.

'The eldest, King Dasaratha's first born and heir.'

'Then he is Raghunatha himself!' cries Lava, falling to his knees with folded hands, tears of happiness in his eyes. 'I am blessed indeed to have been embraced by him today! O father, forgive me for what I just did.'

'What has my child done?' questions Rama gently.

'When he heard the proclamation of your unsurpassed power from the keepers of the sacrificial horse, he challenged them,' said Chandraketu in amusement.

'But such behaviour suits a Kshatriya,' says Rama. 'A man of might does not meekly accept the might of another. It is in his nature to see if he himself can do better. Tell me, son, who endowed you with the secret of the Jrimbhaka missiles? As far as I know, aside from myself and the revered Vashistha, no other living being has been instructed in it.'

'Father, I do not know. These missiles have been available to us from the time of our birth,' replies Lava.

'You use the plural,' notes Rama.

'I have a twin by the name of Kusha.'

'And where is he?' asks Rama, just as Kusha walks up to them with his bow slung over his arm.

'The sight of this child moves me beyond words,' thinks Rama, as he gazes at Kusha.

'Brother, what is this fight I hear of? Who dared challenge you?' asks Kusha of Lava.

'There is no fight. Not anymore. But brother, you must drop your pride, for we are now in the presence of Lord Rama, the king of Raghus.'

'The hero of the *Ramayana*! But how should I greet him?' asks Kusha.

'As you would a father.' And Lava explains to Kusha his connection with Chandraketu. 'Come greet him, brother,' says Lava, steering Kusha towards Rama.

'Don't bow to me,' says Rama, raising the kneeling Kusha. 'My heart swells with fatherly love somehow. Therefore, embrace me.'

As he holds the two boys close to him, Rama wonders, 'Could they be mine? Their close resemblance to Sita with their moon-like faces and soft curls, the same colouring and bearing as myself ... how many times did I place my hand on my beloved's swollen stomach and tell her that I was sure two hearts beat in there instead of one? Even their age fits perfectly with my suspicion. And the Jrimbhaka missiles! Could it be that my blessing to Sita as we saw the painting that distant day has come true? I clearly remember my own words to her: "As of this moment, they will reveal their secrets to the child you are carrying, just as they have revealed them to me."'

'Father, what is it?' asks Lava anxiously, seeing the tears in Rama's eyes.

'Lava, what a silly question you ask,' scolds Kusha gently. 'We know from our study of the *Ramayana* that the loss of his queen has weighed heavily on the king these many years. That has been his one source of constant sorrow. Yet you question him.'

'Oh,' thinks Rama dejectedly, the ray of hope suddenly lessening. 'They speak with such indifference. Surely they can have no connection to Sita then.'

At the sound of approaching feet, Rama looks up. 'It is my mother and the revered Arundhati. But who is accompanying them? Father Janaka! How can I face him? How can I face them all after what I have done to their beloved daughter? Yet I must pay my respects.'

He moves towards them hesitantly. 'Look at the love in Mother Kaushalya's eyes as she sees me,' he thinks. 'Truly, a mother's heart is all forgiving. Now Father Janaka has seen me. Is there anger there? No, only joy and forgiveness. I am spared although God knows I don't deserve to be!'

Rama falls to his knees before these beloved elders.

Lakshmana arrives.

'Greetings to my elders! Long live the king! Your Majesty, the play is about to begin,' says Lakshmana.

'What play, son?' asks Kaushalya.

'Mother, the venerable Valmiki had sent a certain part of the script of his *Ramayana* to sage Bharata to be enacted by the celestial nymphs. That part of the story was revealed to none else. It is now about to be staged, and all the gods, the Kshatriyas, the common people of our kingdom, all have been invited to watch it. The audience is already seated. Now they only await the arrival of the king in order to begin.'

Rising, they follow Lakshmana through the woods to the designated venue. Rama and Lakshmana, Chandraketu, Lava and Kusha, Kaushalya, Janaka and Arundhati all take the seats of honour reserved for them. The play begins.

From behind the curtains comes a soft voice, filled with pain and sorrow. It is a familiar voice. 'Alas, my lord, Lakshmana has gone away and now I am all alone.'

Rama gives a start.

'Abandoned by Rama, overcome by the pangs of childbirth, Sita throws herself into the river,' announces the Sutradhaar.

Hearing this, Rama leaps to his feet. 'Sita! Wait!'

Quickly restraining him, Lakshmana whispers, 'Your Majesty, calm yourself. It is only a play.'

Sita emerges, supported by Ganga and Prithvi, goddess of the Earth and mother of Sita. In their arms are two baby boys. At the sight of his beloved, Rama faints.

'Brother,' begs Lakshmana, although badly shaken himself, 'you must control yourself. There is something the great Valmiki wants to tell the world. We must see what it is.'

Reviving, Rama gets a hold of himself with some difficulty and watches the rest of the play quietly, although his body is wracked by tremors from time to time.

'Sita, child, take heart,' says Ganga. 'Goddess Prithvi, why the tears?'

'How can a mother witness the pain of her beloved daughter and remain unmoved?' asks Prithvi.

'This suffering was in her fate. But she has returned to you, her mother, in her darkest hour. Prithvi, take her away and keep her with you,' instructs Ganga.

'I will take her with me into the heart of the earth. But what of these beautiful twin boys, abandoned by their father before they were even born?'

Here Rama gives a start and looks in the direction of Lava and Kusha. However the twins, unaware of anything unusual, continue to watch the play with great interest.

'Why do you speak in such harsh tones of Rama? Do you not know him well?' questions Ganga of Prithvi.

'I do. Yet my mother's heart cannot forgive what he did to my innocent child.'

'O mother, do not speak of my husband that way,' pleads Sita in distress.

'Your husband? Who do you refer to in that manner, daughter, the man who abandoned you?' demands Prithvi.

'But what else was he to do?' interjects Ganga. 'A scandal had spread among the people of Ayodhya. Sita had passed through fire to prove her innocence but that was in far away Lanka. What were the people here, with their common minds, to believe? Rama's inheritance was the honour and spotless reputation of his race. What choice did he have but to uphold that honour? No Prithvi, you are being unfair to him.'

Prithvi's anger lessens at these words. Somewhat embarrassed, she says, 'It is not as if I do not know Rama's love for Sita. After abandoning my daughter, he has lived by the strength of his mind and great fortitude and for the charitable acts he performs in the interest of his people alone,' she says.

'Mother, the sky is lit up!' cries Sita, looking around her in wonder.

'They are the Jrimbhaka missiles,' explains Prithvi. 'Look, they have landed at the feet of the twins, as if paying respect to them!'

'Ah, my husband!' says Sita happily. 'These are your blessings come true, spoken when I was pregnant as we looked at the paintings!'

Here Rama casts another glance at Lava and Kusha. Now the twins are not as calm as they were before. It appears as if they too have caught on to something, but they are only half-comprehending. They look at each other once, and then quickly turn their attention back to the stage.

'Divine one, who will perform the sacred rites befitting the Kshatriya class for my sons?' asks Sita of Ganga.

'Have no worry on that account, daughter. Give them to me, and I will take them to sage Valmiki. He will raise them as his own and perform the appropriate rites when the time comes.'

Rama's breath catches in his throat. He is unable to move, so great is his joy. When his eyes fall on Lava and Kusha, he finds them both sitting motionless, silent tears running down their faces.

On stage, Sita hands over the two little boys to Mother Ganga, who disappears and reappears a little later without them. 'Mother,' says Sita to Prithvi, 'even my children have gone. I have nothing else to live for. Absorb me into yourself. Put an end to my unhappy life, I beg you.'

'Come, daughter,' says Prithvi. Suddenly the stage and the very earth beneath it part, and Sita is absorbed into it.

'Sita!' cries Rama leaping to his feet, his hand outstretched to her.

'Mother, no!' cry Lava and Kusha together. But it is too late. The small figure of Sita completely disappears, and the earth closes around her.

Then suddenly a voice rings out from backstage: 'Clear the stage! Remove the musical instruments! All you beings, animate and inanimate, behold now a holy miracle ordained by the venerable sage Valmiki ...'

'The waters of the Ganga appear restless and turbulent. The sky—O brother, the skies are filled with divine sages!' observes Lakshmana. Suddenly he gives a cry, 'Look! Mother Sita is emerging from the waters. With her are Ganga and Prithvi.'

Both goddesses speak together. 'Lord of the world, Ramachandra, we hand over to you your virtuous wife, passed through fire once and today through earth and holy water. She is so pure that our own sanctity has increased many times over by touching her! Receive her now and replace the golden statue beside you with her true form.'

Rama comes forward with his hands outstretched towards Sita. His remorse, his love, his prolonged suffering and his joy are all there, written in his eyes.

'Forgive me,' he says brokenly. Unable to bear his pain, Sita grasps his hands, telling him through her tears and her touch that all is forgiven.

'Citizens of Ayodhya,' say the goddesses, 'here is Queen Sita, born of sacrificial ground, and daughter-in-law of the solar dynasty. Vindicated by Fire, Earth and Water, what do you think of accepting her now?'

The audience rises to its feet as one, hands folded, heads bowed with shame. 'Let Kusha and Lava, the sons of Rama and Sita, be presented now,' says Ganga.

The twins turn eagerly to Valmiki, who smiles his consent. With tears of happiness they rush into the arms of their overjoyed parents. As she holds her children close, Sita looks up at Valmiki, sitting somewhere in the audience. Meeting his eyes over hundreds of heads, she folds her hands in gratitude. Valmiki raises his own in blessing.

Silappadikāram

Illanko Adigal

Sanskrit and Greek epics traditionally revolved around great men who fought great wars. But the only wars that are fought in the Tamil epic Silappadikāram *are the struggles with the self. And the hero of this epic is a woman.*

Tamil scholars attribute the Silappadikāram *to Illanko Adigal, the ascetic prince. The word 'Adigal' means 'saint' in Tamil. The* Silappadikāram *is divided into three parts—the Books of Puhar, Madurai and Vanji. The story moves from one to the other of the capitals of the three Tamil kingdoms, the Cholas, Pandyas and Cheras. The unifying force across the books is the exemplary Kannagi.*

When Kovalan leaves his gentle wife Kannagi, her internal war begins. Her silence and self-possession reveal little of the hurt and unhappiness she is suffering.

Silappadikāram means 'story of the anklet'. Kannagi's anklet assumes human-like proportions in the tale. It is the symbol of her purity and indicates her married status. The anklet, which she freely gives to Kovalan when he returns poverty-stricken to her, is an indication of her forgiveness. Finally, it becomes the chief evidence in a trial of murder.

When Kannagi breaks her anklet in the court of the Pandyan king, in essence she unleashes the deadly wrath so far contained within her. The breaking of a girdle or an anklet is symbolic of calamity, not only in this story but also in Biblical narratives. When Kannagi breaks her anklet, it symbolises the doom of Madurai.

In the male-dominated world of epic heroes, Kannagi who wields neither sword nor bow, may be a deviation from the norm. But she is a hero nonetheless. And so she remains one of the best-loved figures of Tamil lore even some 2000 years after she first came into existence.

The Story of an Anklet

Once a chaste woman was wronged by the unjust verdict of a king. Crazed with anguish, she burnt down his capital with the fury of her breast. So says the legend ...

***

In the prosperous city of Puhar lived ancient families—clans that had lived and died in peace and harmony. One such family was Masattuvan's. A rich and generous merchant, he was now busy with the marriage preparations of his son Kovalan to Kannagi, the lovely daughter of his friend Manaykan.

Her skin the colour of beaten gold, Kannagi was beautiful with bow-shaped eyes and a nose as straight as Kama's arrow. Her quiet self-possession, exceptional beauty, delicate figure and quiet modesty made her completely deserving of the praise she received. It was a marriage made in heaven—for Kovalan was handsome, wealthy, impulsive and generous. Above all, he doted on his young bride.

When the marriage ceremony was over, Kovalan took Kannagi back to his family home. With Kannagi came a trousseau of the finest silk clothes and gold jewellery that her mother had collected for her since the day she was born. Most beautiful among the ornaments was a pair of gold anklets. An aged master craftsman from the distant Cheral capital of Vanji had specially made them for Kannagi.

'Why have they decked you so in diamonds and brocade?' asked Kovalan teasingly, taking Kannagi's hand and drawing her to his side on the flower-bedecked nuptial bed. 'Your slender frame can scarcely bear their weight.' And Kovalan removed each ornament, flower and bit of clothing from his bride's body ...

The months passed in a haze of love. Kovalan took delight in troubling his shy wife. He would chase her noisily across the terraces of his home and draw pictures of deer and flowers with sandalwood paste on her shoulders. This would embarrass the demure and serious Kannagi, who was ever aware that Kovalan's parents could hear them at play. But her pleas and entreaties only inspired Kovalan to further mischief.

'Our son will never grow up!' sighed Kovalan's mother, shaking her head.

'Let him be,' replied Masattuvan gently. 'Soon they will move to a home of their own. We must enjoy their presence while we can.'

Masattuvan and his wife were building a separate house for the young couple. When it was complete, they furnished it with richly carved pillars and bedposts, stocked it with polished silver and gleaming brass vessels, and filled it with every comfort that a young couple could desire. In the meanwhile Kannagi had quietly followed her mother-in-law about the house, lending an attentive ear to her many instructions on the running of a household. She had learnt quickly.

Finally the day came when Kovalan and Kannagi left the house of Masattuvan, and accompanied by a retinue of servants, entered their own home. Days turned into months and months into years. They lived together in perfect understanding and joy, entwined like two snakes lost in each other.

Kannagi, the most skilled among housewives, cooked delicious food for her husband, kept the lamps burning and the house fragrant with flowers. She received her guests graciously, gave alms to the poor, and thereby brought honour on her kinsmen. For all her youth she was upheld as foremost among the virtuous women of Puhar. Yet she remained as modest and simple as the day she first set foot as a child-bride in her husband's home.

In the street of the dancers and courtesans lived a young woman named Madhavi. It seemed as if the blessings of the gods had come together in her face and form. Saraswati herself danced when Madhavi donned her anklets, and surely, none other than Kamadeva must have groomed her in the art of love! Her ambitious mother Chitrapati had carefully watched over Madhavi. Madhavi's exuberance and beauty were enhanced by her lust for life, her ability to debate with the best, and her natural wit and charm.

The time had come for Madhavi's first dance performance. The king himself had promised to attend. Chitrapati, with the help of learned men, inspected the soil upon which the stage was to be erected. The site chosen, she went on to design the stage, dropping strings of rare pearls as a backdrop until they formed a solid glowing curtain. A thousand lamps lit up the stage, making it impossible to tell whether it was day or night.

Finally the day of the performance arrived.

Kannagi entered the chamber she shared with Kovalan to find him getting dressed. Turning, he drew her into his arms.

'I'm heading to the dance performance of a maiden named Madhavi. She is the daughter of the famous dancer Chitrapati. Have you heard of her?' asked Kovalan. Kannagi nodded. The string of jasmines in her thick braid brushed against his nose and he inhaled appreciatively.

'It is said that they are the descendants of the celestial nymph Urvashi,' went on Kovalan.

'Then she must be a beautiful dancer!' exclaimed Kannagi, her eyes wide with wonder.

'That remains to be seen,' replied Kovalan, looking down at his wife and marvelling yet again at her innocent loveliness.

Kannagi went downstairs with her husband and saw him off at the front door of their home. She watched him walk away from her down the busy street. Then she turned and re-entered the house, closing the doors quietly behind her.

The stage was ready. The lamps were lit. Madhavi had been dressed with the greatest care by the most skilful of hands. She glowed like a goddess. The king took his place on the seat of honour; then the courtiers, the important people of Puhar (among them Kovalan), the patrons of the arts, and finally the commoners. When the murmur of the crowd had quietened to a hush and the bells had rung to signify the start of the performance, the musicians took their places on the stage. Finally, placing her right foot forward, Madhavi stepped out. The audience drew in a collective breath, spellbound by her loveliness!

The music rang out and Madhavi forgot herself. She forgot her audience, her trepidation, the rules of dance. She was only aware of the music, and her body was a flowing, tangible manifestation of that music. She danced on through folk styles, classical styles, and sometimes a fusion of the two. The gods in their heavens stopped to watch her; the peacocks in the hills beyond lowered their splendid tails in defeat.

At the end of the performance, the king stood up and bestowed upon Madhavi a flower garland and one thousand and eight pieces of gold. She had been acknowledged as the finest dancer in Puhar!

After the king and his courtiers left, the people slowly ebbed away from the arena like waves at low tide. The lamps around the stage were extinguished, the flowers and pearls removed, and the place was almost in darkness. Only one man remained in the arena, rooted to his seat. Kovalan.

Kovalan had lost his heart to the dancer Madhavi. Kovalan, the beloved of Kannagi.

Back in her quarters, Madhavi summoned her trusted maid Vasantamalai.

'Go down to the street below and tell the rich and noble men of Puhar that the highest bidder of this garland shall be my lord.'

Vasantamalai left to do her mistress's bidding. Within minutes a crowd had gathered around her in the street. The price for the garland soared higher and higher. Suddenly, Kovalan stepped forward and named a price. And such a price it was! Unimaginable, incomparable! Kovalan himself didn't seem to realise what he had just done. In a daze he claimed the garland and entered Madhavi's house. As he took her in his arms, he gave himself to her heart and soul, sparing nothing for the gentle, innocent wife waiting for him at home.

That night and the day after that, Kannagi watched at her window for her husband's return. But she listened in vain for his familiar step. Her initial surprise turned to fear for his safety. But when the truth burst forth from the frenzied lips of her maid recently arrived from the marketplace, Kannagi sank to the floor in stunned despair. She could not understand why her adoring husband of two days before had left her for another woman. Her heart cried out in anguish, but she stilled it, not wanting to be disloyal to Kovalan even in thought. So, with her characteristic forbearance, Kannagi silently set aside her grief and went about her days following her old routine. Looking at her no one could tell how she suffered inside. Her home remained clean and calm, a haven to the seekers of alms—as if its master had never deserted it and gone away.

The good Masattuvan and his wife came hurrying to their daughter-in-law's side as soon as they heard the news. Kannagi received them with respect and affection, showing none of her grief. She did not want to let Kovalan down in front of his parents, or to increase their sorrow with her own. She was deeply moved by their concern for her. And while she went about being normal for their benefit, in her heart she clung to them more than ever before. The poor parents, ashamed of their son's behaviour, unable to break through Kannagi's reserve, went away bewildered and sad.

Meanwhile Kovalan and Madhavi were lost in love. The world beyond their front door ceased to exist. What charms did the quiet and serious Kannagi hold before Madhavi's vibrant beauty and tinkling laughter? She was as spontaneous as Kannagi was reserved, as remarkable as Kannagi was self-effacing. The years with Madhavi passed happily, and Kannagi was completely obliterated from Kovalan's mind.

Kovalan spared nothing to please Madhavi. He spent money lavishly, fulfilling her every desire. Generous by nature, his delight in Madhavi made him benevolent to the world in general. He gave freely and impulsively to the deserving and the undeserving alike. He never returned to his father's business, and soon began to draw on his sizable inheritance to keep up his lifestyle. But like everything that is finite, his wealth too began to dwindle. There came a time when, with despair he realised that he wasn't the wealthy young man he had once been.

It was a courtesan's job to procure for herself a wealthy patron and sustain his interest until a wealthier one came along. But Madhavi was truly in love with Kovalan. His change in fortunes did little to diminish her passion for him. In her own way she was as devoted to him as Kannagi was.

It was the time of the Indra festival, when this god was propitiated with sacrifices, splendid processions, music and dance. As Puhar's most promising dancer, Madhavi was the centre of attention. Her dancing had become even more graceful over the years. The pleasure she took in her art and in Kovalan enhanced her outward perfection with an inner radiance. Now in the days of the festival, all eyes were turned on her.

On the last day of the festival, Kovalan was sulking from a lover's quarrel and Madhavi badly wanted to placate him. That night she dressed with special care, oiling and washing her luxuriant hair with herbs, decorating her feet with red lac and tinkling anklets, and her wrists with dancing bracelets. Over her waist and loins she draped silken cloths and a pearl-studded girdle. When she entered their bedchamber with swaying gait, Kovalan was captivated.

Climbing onto a prettily erected dais, Madhavi beckoned to Kovalan to join her. She did not realise that his irritation at the quarrel, forgotten momentarily, had returned to nag him. Her regal gesture, the way she expected him to come at her bidding, rankled him further.

'Does she forget I am a man? Perhaps she is intoxicated by the adulation of the people,' he thought, even as he climbed the dais and took his place. Then, unexpectedly came the thought, 'Kannagi never demanded anything. I was her lord and as such did she treat me!'

Unaware of this growing irritation, Madhavi tuned up the lute and began to play. She was splendid that night, probably because she forgot the world and played only for Kovalan. She played with all the love in her heart.

'My lord, won't you sing to me?' she asked.

Kovalan, who himself had an excellent voice, sang. Another command! The slight tremor in his voice, born from anger, Madhavi mistook for love. She was completely carried away by his song. It was a love song, but it ended with the bitter lines:

Stay clear of her o lovely swan, your gait is unlike hers!
She wanders the world inflaming it, only to leave it
Like the receding waters of the swirling waves.
Stay clear of her o lovely swan, your gait is unlike hers!

'Are his unkind words directed at me?' thought Madhavi bewildered. 'Does he wish to insinuate that I am dishonest and untrue to him?'

But she hid her pain behind a bright smile and took up the challenge. Tuning the lute again, she sang a song in answer to his. Her theme was about a lonely woman who remained true to her lover even after he had left her. She wanted to assure Kovalan that should he turn his back on her, there would be no room for another in her heart. Her song went like this:

A man came from a distant land
And wrecked our happy games!
He wrecked our games and went away
Without a backward glance.
Yet this faithless man will not leave my heart!
Oh friend with jasmines in your hair, tell me,
Now that the birdsong has ended and the sun faded away,
Will the darkness that envelops my heart
Follow him to the land where he has gone?

This was the nail in the coffin of their relationship. Kovalan rose to his feet and looked down at Madhavi, his eyes blazing. 'She has fallen in love with another man,' he thought furiously. 'Look how she pines for him! Her lyrics were intended to convey that my attentions are no longer welcome. Only, she cannot speak straight. It is in the blood of her kind to manipulate men with words. After all, she is a courtesan!'

Madhavi did not hear his words for he spoke them only in thought. But she read the anger in his eyes and knew that somehow he had misunderstood her song. The disgust on his face cut her to the heart. Before she could compose herself, Kovalan mounted his horse and rode away.

Madhavi slowly made her way back home. As she mounted the steps and entered her bedchamber alone, the numbness inside gave way to terrible despair. She lay on the bed a long time, pain washing over her in waves.

'Poor Kannagi too must have suffered this way when he turned away from her,' she thought remorsefully.

But as the hours went by, Madhavi's natural optimism returned. 'If he loved me once he can love me again. This is just a misunderstanding. I will send him a message and he will surely come back home.'

Madhavi combed and oiled her thick hair and bound it up with flowers. She donned her best ornaments. The mirror told her she was beautiful. Gathering the freshest flowers from her garden, she wove them into a garland. On the petals of the white screw pine she inscribed the words:

> Spring has come to reunite the hearts of those in love.
> It is true that Kama will punish with his arrows of
> flowers
> Lovers who have loved and parted.
> I trust you understand my meaning, my lord.
> – Madhavi

Calling Vasantamalai, she asked her to find Kovalan and give him her message along with the garland. Vasantamalai was glad to do anything she could to help her mistress. She was terrified by the changes that grief had brought to Madhavi in a few short hours. She hurried away, stopping often to enquire after Kovalan's whereabouts. She found him in the street of the grain merchants.

'Sir, my mistress has sent you this garland. Please read her words and return home,' she said, offering the garland to him.

Kovalan smiled and Vasantamalai took heart. 'Your mistress first performed the dance of the meeting eyes and I was captivated. The kumkum on her forehead, the anklets at her feet stole my heart away—she danced the dance of love. The flowers in her hair, her coral lips spoke of her love for me to every passerby—she performed the dance of revelation. So beautiful she was! And all these dances added to her glow ... for after all, she is only a dancing girl.'

He spoke so pleasantly that it took a moment for Vasantamalai to catch the derision in his last words. Shocked and grieved she held out the garland, wordlessly pleading with him to read Madhavi's message. But he walked away without even touching it.

Vasantamalai returned home and tearfully told her mistress what had happened. Although Madhavi said cheerfully, 'He is only angry. Surely he will return in the morning,' an icy loneliness seeped into her heart and she knew that Kovalan would never come home to her again.

Kannagi was asleep when a terrible dream abruptly woke her up. Rushing downstairs, Kannagi grasped her friend Devandi's hand and cried, 'My husband is in danger!'

'Calm yourself, Kannagi. It was only a dream,' said Devandi, seating Kannagi down and fetching her a cool glass of buttermilk from the kitchen. When Kannagi had drunk it and become herself again, Devandi said gently, 'Kovalan does not dislike you. You are separated from him now because of a vow you failed to keep for him in a previous birth. It is said that women who offer prayers at the temple of Kama near the place where the Kaveri meets the sea will enjoy this world with their husbands. Then they will be reborn in heaven and enjoy the pleasures there. I have recently been to that temple and offered prayers on your behalf. You'll see, Kovalan will return to you.'

Before either of them could say anything more, a maid came rushing into the room crying, 'My lady, the master has come home!'

As Devandi smiled and went away, Kovalan appeared at the door. Kannagi jumped to her feet, her heart beating fast, her usually serene eyes glittering with emotion.

'I left you for a deceitful woman, a charmer of men. Today I return to you with nothing. My wealth is gone, my youth has passed me by, my reputation is in tatters. Kannagi, knowing all this do you still have room for me in your heart and home?' asked Kovalan quietly.

The first smile in many years lit Kannagi's face. Bending down she slipped off one of the pair of priceless anklets that her parents had given her at the time of her marriage. She held it out to Kovalan, and said in a voice that was devoid of reproach, 'Take this, Lord. Then we will not be poor anymore.'

Kovalan's eyes filled with tears. Drawing his wife into his arms, he held her close and wept. His tears mingled with hers. They stood that way for a long time, washing away the sorrow and remorse of the years gone by.

After a while, Kovalan looked down at Kannagi. Her hair was un-oiled and no flowers adorned the silken tresses. Her marriage pendant was her only ornament. And yet, years of suffering had left the innocence in her eyes untouched, adding only dignity and an inner strength that belied her slightness of frame.

'How I have made her suffer!' thought Kovalan. 'What I gave up for titillation and momentary pleasures of the flesh! Losing my wealth would have been the least of my misfortunes had this good woman refused to forgive me, wicked fool that I am!'

Aloud he said, 'Kannagi, come away with me. There is nothing left for me here. I cannot face my parents or yours until I have re-established myself in a respectable business and recovered my wealth. They say Madurai is a prosperous city and the king is just. Let us leave Puhar and begin a new life together there.'

Without a word, Kannagi got up and followed Kovalan out of the security of her home. It was still the hour of darkness. They left with only the clothes on their backs, for they did not want to burden themselves with anything more on the arduous journey that lay ahead.

This was Kovalan's karma leading them by their hand, closer and closer to their destiny. They did not know it, but Kannagi's dream had been the writing on the wall ...

They walked through the streets of Puhar and made their way past the ghats where young women bathed. They passed the five Buddhist temples built by Indra and walked along the riverbank. On the way they saw the royal park whose lake was fragrant with lotuses. Going westwards they walked ten miles until they reached a serene hut in the middle of thick trees.

'Where is Madurai? Are we nearly there?' asked Kannagi, looking up at her husband.

With a smile Kovalan replied, 'Yes, nearly. Only three hundred miles to go.'

Kannagi's eyes widened but she did not complain, merely nodded her head. Kovalan saw the beads of sweat upon her brow, her slender waist, the heaving of her breast. He realised for the first time what he had asked of this delicate creature.

'How sore her feet must be!' he thought. 'Poor girl, she came with me without question because I asked her to, turning her back on her family and the comfort of home. How will she complete such a journey?'

At that moment the door of the hut opened and the ascetic Kavundi emerged. Kovalan and Kannagi went to her and paid their respects.

'You appear to be from a good home. What is your reason for venturing so far from it?'

'Revered one, I wish to seek my fortune in Madurai, having lost everything in Puhar.'

'You intend to undertake this dangerous journey on foot with such a delicate girl in tow?' asked Kavundi, her eyes filling with concern as she appraised Kannagi standing quietly behind her husband. 'Her tiny feet will not be able to bear the thorns of the forests and the pebbles on the road.'

Kannagi looked up then. In her eyes Kavundi saw the indomitable courage that ran through her like a blade of steel. She saw, too, that the karma of this young couple was taking them to Madurai.

'If I were to ask you to turn back you will not, for your mind is made up. For some years now I have had a desire to go to Madurai and listen to the word of dharma from the holy sages there. I have much to learn from them. Hence I will accompany you on this journey. Shall we leave now?'

Kovalan bowed to her with folded hands and said, 'Holy one, if you were to come with us then I shall have no fears for my wife. In your company no harm will ever come to her. Thank you a thousand times!'

'We will have to face the blistering heat if we walk by day. If we walk by night we will face the problem of thorns, snakes, and false pits dug by men. Make up your mind to this and we can be on our way.'

Those few words of Kavundi summed up their gruelling journey to Madurai. For weeks they walked. Kovalan had his strength to sustain him and Kavundi her penance. But nothing could have got Kannagi through that journey except for her single-minded devotion to her husband. At long last the three of them crossed the river and entered the forests on the outskirts of Madurai. By now Kannagi was trembling from exhaustion. Her small feet were red and sore with blisters. She said nothing, but Kovalan and Kavundi could see that she wouldn't be able to take much more.

When they reached a village just outside the gates of Madurai, Kovalan said to Kavundi, 'Holy one, will you remain with Kannagi while I go on to Madurai and make arrangements for our stay? We will rest here during the day and I will set out in the evening to avoid the heat.'

At that moment a humble old herdswoman, Maadari, approached Kavundi and fell at her feet. 'Revered saint, our city is blessed by your presence. You and your companions look tired. Please come to my home and rest there.'

Kavundi looked at Maadari and thought to herself, 'This woman is virtuous and kind. I see no harm in leaving Kannagi in her care.'

'I am accustomed to hardships and have no need of rest,' replied Kavundi. 'But this young girl is exhausted from days of walking. She is a girl from a noble and high-standing family, and I entrust her to your care. Take her and her husband to your home until they find a place of their own.'

Blessing Kovalan, Kannagi and Maadari, Kavundi went on her way.

Maadari was kindness itself. She had a young daughter called Aiyai at home, and felt a similar love for the beautiful Kannagi. She took the young couple to her house. Calling out to Aiyai, she said, 'Treat this girl as a sister. Bathe her feet in cool water and salve, wash her hair with perfumed herbs and dress her in ornaments. Then help her prepare a good meal for her husband.' Turning to Kannagi and Kovalan, she said, 'We have few riches in this home, but everything that we have is yours. Let your stay here be comfortable and happy.'

After a bath, Kannagi prepared a delicious meal for Kovalan with vegetables grown in Maadari's garden. Refreshed and rested, Kovalan took the precious anklet from Kannagi and set out for Madurai. As he walked past a grove of madhavi flowers, he heard someone speaking as if to himself, 'O madhavi flower, you have withered away in the heat like your lotus-eyed namesake when she was parted from her Kovalan!'

Kovalan stopped and turned around in surprise. The speaker was a young Brahmin who was watching him keenly.

'What did you say?' asked Kovalan approaching him.

As he drew nearer the Brahmin, the latter became

excited. 'My search is over! I wasn't sure it was you but now I am.'

'Who are you?' asked Kovalan.

'My name is Kaushikan. After you left Puhar, Madhavi grew pale and ill and took to her bed. She became like a snake that had lost its jewel. Word reached her that I was about to undertake a pilgrimage to Madurai. When she heard from Vasantamalai that Madurai was your destination too, she sent for me and begged me to carry a message to you.' Kaushikan handed a palm leaf to Kovalan, on which Madhavi had written:

'My lord, I implore you to free me of my pain. Please, return to me ...'

Kovalan was moved. He suddenly realised that he had been guilty of misjudging the depth of not one but two women's love for him.

'What a wretch I am!' he thought with self-loathing. 'Some men go to their death without ever knowing the love of a good woman. I was blessed twice over and I did not know it. Yet each of these women has forgiven and loved me without questions or accusations.'

Seeing Kovalan read the palm leaf with tears in his eyes, Kaushikan said, 'Kovalan, don't cry and listen to the good news I bring you. Madhavi has given birth to your daughter. She is a beautiful child, blessed by the Gods! Her mother has entrusted her spiritual care to the great sage Aravana Adigal.'

'Madhavi could have done no better by our child! O, how I long to hold my daughter in my arms, watch her laugh, hear her childish babble. God willing, someday I will return to Puhar to do just that. Kaushikan, bestow one last act of kindness upon me. When you return to Puhar, ask Madhavi to name our child Manimekalai. That is the name of my clan's patron goddess. She is the goddess of the sea and is dear to me!'

Kaushikan promised to deliver Kovalan's message and took leave of him. Kovalan continued on his way. As he entered the capital of the Pandyan king, he heard chanting and bells, rhythmic drumbeats and the auspicious blowing of conches from the temples beyond. The roar of the mighty sea was like a background score to the lives of the people here. The marketplace overflowed with spices and gold, vegetables and silks. This was clearly a land of plenty, one that had known only the benevolence of the gods.

At the street of the goldsmiths Kovalan saw the King's master craftsman dressed in state attire, followed by his retinue of apprentices. 'He will be the best man to fairly estimate the price of my anklet! Besides, there is no fear of him cheating me. Surely the official goldsmith of the fair-minded Pandyan king would be as honest as the king himself,' reckoned Kovalan.

He was wrong.

Approaching the chief goldsmith with folded hands, Kovalan said, 'I have an anklet fit for a queen. Would you tell me how much it will fetch me?'

The goldsmith looked down at the anklet in Kovalan's hands and his eyes widened for an instant. It was the exact replica of the pair of anklets the queen had in her collection—one of which the chief goldsmith himself had stolen! Now the search for the missing anklet was in full swing and the goldsmith had started to grow very nervous.

'I have found my scapegoat!' thought the evil fellow. Masking his cunning behind an ingratiating smile, he said humbly, 'A craftsman far better than myself has made this exquisite ornament. Indeed it should grace the feet of no one but the Queen. Please wait here in my humble home. I will inform His Majesty and return shortly.'

Hurrying to the palace, the goldsmith requested an urgent audience with the king. The Pandyan king was in the Queen's quarters trying to pacify her after a quarrel. The goldsmith entered looking flushed and excited. 'Your majesty! I have found the thief of the stolen anklet! Convincing him that I wish to help him, I have kept him waiting in my house.'

The king and queen leapt to their feet. Sending for three able-bodied guards, the king said, 'Follow the master craftsman and examine the anklet in that man's possession. If indeed it belongs to the queen, behead him instantly!'

No deliberation, no witnesses, no trial. This was the Pandyan king's one obvious chance to placate his wife by restoring the precious anklet to her, and he grabbed it. It was his first and only indiscretion in his many years as king. It would prove to be a costly one.

Back in Maadari's house, Aiyai was preparing to make butter. It was their turn to supply the royal kitchen that day, but for some reason the milk had not curdled.

'A bad omen,' said Maadari worriedly, just as a humped bull passed that way. Kannagi did not know it, but this too was inauspicious. When the cows began to grow restless and the bells slipped from their necks, Aiyai let out a cry, for this was usually a forerunner to a catastrophe. Kannagi didn't quite understand what was going on, but a feeling of terrible foreboding had settled upon her.

Taking matters into her hands, Maadari said to Aiyai, 'Don't be upset. We must stay calm, for we are scaring our gentle guest. Call all the young maidens of our village and let us distract ourselves with the round dance of Krishna and his gopikas.'

Seating Kannagi on a mat under a shady tree and herself beside her, Maadari indicated for the girls to begin the dance. The cows settled down and for a while peace was restored in Kannagi's heart.

Meanwhile the chief goldsmith followed by the king's guards made their way back to the house where Kovalan was waiting. 'These are the king's men,' said the goldsmith to Kovalan. 'Show them the anklet so that they may decide a price.'

Innocent of the trap his own fate had laid for him, Kovalan unwrapped the anklet. There was a collective gasp. No doubt this was the very same anklet that had belonged to the queen! Quickly drawing the goldsmith aside the guards said, 'The evidence damns him. Yet his noble bearing and straightforward manner contradict our suspicion.'

'Fools!' thought the goldsmith. They are going to ruin everything! But he did not reveal his desperation. Instead he said calmly, 'How else could he have come into possession of the anklet? Without tools and weapons, with only the use of sleep-inducing spells, this man has made the Queen's guards drowsy and stolen the anklet from under their noses. Such is his cunning! Now you too have fallen under his spell. Wake up! You know the king's orders. It is not for you to use your judgement.'

Stung by the insinuation that they were gullible, the third guard spun around and wrenched the anklet from the surprised Kovalan's hand. At the same instant the second guard struck out at him with his sword, making a clear gash across his throat. Blood gushed out in torrents from the open wound. Kovalan fell to the ground, dead.

At that instant the sceptre of the great Pandyan, descendant of a line of kings known for their unblemished rule, bent out of shape.

The dance having ended, one of the herdswomen went down to the river to worship the goddess Netumal with flowers and incense. Within minutes she came rushing back, her eyes wild, her hair dishevelled. She stood before Kannagi, not saying a word.

Kannagi rose to her feet and stared at the herdswoman.

The foreboding in her heart returned, growing until it threatened to choke her. Suddenly she looked around her, her eyes frantically searching, 'Where is my husband? He should have come home by now!'

Sensing something terrible, Maadari put a hand on Kannagi's arm to calm her. But Kannagi shook her off and ran to the herdswoman, taking her by the shoulders and crying, 'My heart knows something that my mind doesn't yet understand. I'm in turmoil! What has happened? Tell me, I beg you!'

'Your husband was accused of stealing the queen's anklet and put to death,' said the herdswoman.

For a moment Kannagi stood still, and her face turned white. Then she fainted. Maadari, Aiyai and the other herdswomen, almost weeping with pity, rushed about trying to revive her. When she came around, Kannagi rose to her feet and cried out, 'O my Kovalan, my beloved, where are you? They have stolen you from me, and now I am alone! What should I do? Should I sit beside your funeral pyre and take painful vows like other women do? Must I suffer in silence and be ruined because of the injustice of a king? Till this moment I have borne my fate uncomplainingly. Now, no more! Tell me, o sun! You, who sees everything thing that happens in this world, is my husband a thief?'

'He is not a thief,' spoke a voice from the sky. 'This city will pay for the sin of killing an innocent man!'

Stopping only to snatch up the remaining anklet in her

possession, her beautiful hair billowing around her face, her beautiful eyes red and blazing, Kannagi ran out into the street. Seeing this angry, distraught woman, the people of Madurai were anxious and depressed.

Kannagi didn't stop until she reached the palace. There she found the queen sitting by her husband's side, her good humour restored by the precious anklet.

'O guard, tell your unjust king that the true owner of the anklet demands to see him!'

When the king received this message he was puzzled. 'Sounds like a raving lunatic,' he said. 'Show her in.'

The guard led Kannagi into the courtroom and presented her before the king. At the sight of her the Pandyan was moved. 'Good woman, who are you? Tell me what your trouble is and I will do everything in my power to help.'

'You have already tested your power to its limits, O impetuous king! Now hear me. Kovalan, son of the merchant prince Masattuvan of Puhar, came to make his fortune in Madurai. Using as capital the money he received from the sale of my anklet, he was to start his business. When he entered the city to sell the anklet in good faith he was murdered. I am Kannagi, his widow.'

'Madam,' said the Pandyan gently, 'it is not unjust to slay a thief. You should know that it is a king's duty.'

'My husband was not a thief. I gave him my anklet of my own free will. That anklet rightfully belonged to me.'

'You will have to prove it.'

'That I will. My anklet is filled with rubies,' said Kannagi.

'And ours is filled with pearls. Getting down to the truth of the matter should be easy enough,' said the Pandiyan. 'Present the queen's anklet!'

The guards brought it on a silver tray. Bending down Kannagi unclasped her remaining anklet and laid it beside the other one. They were clearly two of a pair. The king began to grow slightly alarmed. A tense murmur filled the court. The queen looked on anxiously.

Lifting the anklet that the guards had seized from Kovalan, Kannagi hurled it to the ground, breaking it open with one stroke. Hundreds of rubies leaped into the air and scattered across the floor. A horrified silence fell upon the court. The king went white. Glancing down at the sceptre in his hand, he saw that it was bent.

'What sort of a king am I?' he cried. 'I listened to the words of my evil goldsmith and killed an innocent man without even a trial. It is not the goldsmith who has sinned, it is I! I have failed my people and my sceptre. What use is my life then? Let it crumble in the dust.'

The Pandyan slumped to the floor, dead. The queen rose to her feet. 'There is only one recourse for a woman who has lost her husband,' she wept. Softly holding her husband's feet, she too gave up her life.

'My retribution doesn't end here!' cried Kannagi, turning on the stunned courtiers. And wrenching off her left breast, she ran out into the streets, circling the city of Madurai three times before hurling it at the ground, crying, 'O Madurai of the four temples, I curse you. Your king sinned in killing the man I love!'

As she spoke, Agni, the god of fire, appeared before her.

'Kannagi,' he said, 'long ago I knew that I was meant to burn down Madurai the day you were wronged. I await only your instructions. Whom to consume and whom to spare?'

Even in her terrible grief, the gentle faces of Maadari, Aiyai and the herdswomen sprang to Kannagi's mind. 'Spare the good people, the cattle and the innocent. But destroy the wicked,' she said.

Agni rose and billowed out, spreading himself everywhere. Flames shot up into the sky, fanned by raging winds. In this inferno, the glorious city of Madurai burned to the ground ...

Desolate now that her rage was spent, Kannagi left the city by its western gates. She walked for many days without awareness of heat, fatigue, hunger or thirst. Finally, without even knowing it, she entered the Cheral capital of Vanji.

At the foothills of a mountain, Kannagi suddenly heard her name being called. She looked up and saw Kovalan! He was no more in his earthly form, but his spirit stood there, glowing and radiant, surrounded by the gods. With a cry, Kannagi reached out her arms to him. Before the stunned eyes of the nearby hill dwellers, the gods themselves came down to earth, lifted Kannagi and took her away to heaven so that she could rejoin her husband.

'This is a miracle!' cried one of the hill dwellers.

'We must tell the king,' said another.

The reigning king at that time was Senguttavan, known for his valour and courage in battle. When the hill dwellers reported what they had seen, a visiting poet, Cattan, suddenly stood up in court and spoke.

'I know who this woman is. She is Kannagi of one breast, the chaste wife of Kovalan.' He told the king the story as we know it. He also told the king something as yet unknown.

'Kovalan's father, when he heard what became of his son and daughter-in-law, gave away all his wealth and entered the Jain monastery. His dear friend Manaykan, Kannagi's father, did the same. Neither of the mothers recovered from their loss. They both died shortly after they received the news. Madhavi was heartbroken when she heard of Kovalan's death. To the consternation of her mother Chitrapati, she put away her anklets and her lute, and sought refuge in Aravana Adigal, the great Jain monk to whose care she had already entrusted Manimekalai.

'Meanwhile, O king, the fire at Madurai had spared Maadari, Aiyai and their kinswomen. But Maadari threw herself in the fire crying, "I have no right to live after I failed to protect the innocent Kannagi who was left in my care!" and she immolated herself.'

'The Pandyan has sinned indeed!' cried Senguttavan.

Turning to his queen he asked, 'Which of the two women do you think is the greater—Kannagi who avenged her husband's death or the Pandiyan queen who followed her husband in it?'

Senguttavan's wife had been deeply moved by Cattan's story. Her eyes swimming with tears, she replied, 'There is no doubt the Pandiyan's wife was chaste and blessed. Her love and devotion to her husband will surely win her a place in heaven. But Kannagi is, beyond doubt, a goddess. My lord, let us build a temple to her and worship her as the goddess of Chastity.'

'You have spoken well,' replied Senguttavan. 'We shall do as you say. The stone from which the goddess' image is carved shall come from the Himalayas. It shall be bathed in the holy Ganga. Let us set out for the North country immediately.'

Three years it took Senguttavan to carry out his mission. The kings of the North were hostile, and challenged him in battle. Senguttavan was ready. He defeated them all and returned home with the sacred stone in his arms.

An image of Kannagi, the goddess of Chastity, was carved out of the stone by the finest craftsmen, and installed in the shrine. Around its neck was the sacred marriage pendant. On one foot, carved from the same stone, was a single, exquisite anklet ...

Manimekalai

Sattanar

Manimekalai *is the sequel to* Silappadikāram, *and was written by Sattanar of Madurai, a contemporary and friend of Illanko Adigal. It was a product of the Sangam era, sometime between the third and sixth centuries* AD. *Tamil is one of the world's oldest languages. However, it is the only one that is still widely spoken, long after its contemporaries receded into the annals of ancient texts and treatises.*

The Silappadikāram *culminates with the deification of Kannagi as the goddess of Chastity. Kovalan is dead and Madurai burnt down by Kannagi's wrath. From this point* Manimekalai *takes us back to serene Puhar, the place where it all began. We are now introduced to young Manimekalai, Kovalan's daughter through the courtesan Madhavi.*

At this time Buddhism and Jainism were flourishing under the Hindu rule of the Cholas, Pandyas and Cheras. So it is not surprising that an epic like Manimekalai, *based on the tenets of Buddhist* philosophy, came into being. What is remarkable, however, is that the central figure is a young, illegitimate girl born into a courtesan's family. This story is about Manimekalai's struggle against her desires and attachments. It tells of her journey to self-realisation.

From his writings it is fairly safe to assume that Sattanar was staunchly Buddhist, and championed its teachings. Manimekalai, like Silappadikāram, is a treasure trove of information about life, art, culture and society of the Tamils of the Sangam era.

The Dancer and the Begging Bowl

Puhar. The seat of the Chola Kings. The land of Kannagi and Kovalan. This is where the story of Manimekalai too unfolded.

Manimekalai was the child of Kovalan and the courtesan Madhavi. She was her mother's equal in beauty as well as in dance and music. But in piety and forbearance she was like Kannagi, whom she looked upon as a second mother. There was no jealousy in Madhavi's heart. She believed the wife of her dead lover Kovalan to be virtuous and good. Again and again she told Manimekalai of how Kannagi's righteous anger over Kovalan's murder had burnt the Pandya capital of Madurai to ashes.

When Kovalan died, a distraught Madhavi sought consolation at the feet of the great sage Aravana Adigal. His words changed the course of her life.

'Your sorrow is a consequence of birth and rebirth.'

'O Sage, how does one end sorrow?' asked Madhavi, not understanding.

'By breaking free of the cycle of birth and death. Give up all attachments and desires,' replied the sage.

Madhavi took his words to heart and shared them with Manimekalai.

That year, during the Indra festival, when Puhar invited its most skilled dancers, neither Madhavi nor Manimekalai appeared. Not even Madhavi's mother Chitrapati's command could summon them. They remained in their simple quarters with their companion Sudhamati, stringing flowers for the evening prayers.

As they sat, Madhavi recounted the story of Kannagi and Kovalan. Hearing it, Manimekalai began to weep.

'Manimekalai,' said Madhavi, gently wiping her daughter's face. 'Your tears have fallen on the flowers. Go out and fetch some more.'

As Manimekalai got up to leave, Sudhamati leaped to her feet.

'Let me accompany her, Madhavi! If she goes alone, she will be waylaid by the eager townspeople. I know of a lovely garden called Uvavana. It is unfrequented, and within its walls live birds of every kind. The rarest and most beautiful flowers are found there in abundance, and in the heart of the garden, inside a crystal pavilion, there is a shrine dedicated to Lord Buddha. We will go there to gather the flowers.'

As the two young women made their way through the streets of Puhar, Manimekalai was greeted by many. Some reproached Madhavi for forcing an ascetic's life on so lovely a girl. Others recalled how gifted a dancer Manimekalai was. But Manimekalai walked on quietly, indifferent to the glances and comments about her.

Uvavana was even more beautiful than Sudhamati's description. How can words do justice to a place that remains serene in the middle of the hustle of mundane living, silent when the air is full of birdsong? Manimekalai and Sudhamati entered the splendid garden. They did not know that fast on their heels was Udayakumaran, prince and heir to the Chola Empire.

Udayakumaran was as brave and handsome as Lord Murugan himself, and was loved by his people. The young man had long ago lost his heart to Manimekalai.

When the sound of chariot wheels reached Manimekalai, she cried, 'Sudhamati! I think Prince Udayakumaran has followed me here. My grandmother Chitrapati has often tried to coax me into accepting him. She claims that his heart is set on me. What shall I do? How shall I escape him?'

Manimekalai was afraid she would be forced to submit to the prince if he found her. But she was also alarmed by her deep and inexplicable longing to see him. Why she felt so drawn to him she could not understand. But she instinctively knew that if she saw him she might forget her chosen path and willingly become his.

'Go inside the crystal pavilion and lock the door,' urged Sudhamati. 'Hurry!'

Within seconds of Manimekalai bolting the door of the pavilion, Udayakumaran was upon Sudhamati. Without preamble he asked, 'Where is she? I am not fooled by your standing alone. She is here somewhere. Tell me where she is! Tell me why she has left the street where her family lives!'

Sudhamati answered quietly, 'O prince, calm down and listen to me carefully. You of noble blood should understand better than others that to pursue a pious woman is a sin. Manimekalai has chosen to renounce the world and spend her life in search of spiritual salvation. Do not persist in engaging her affections. She may be young, but she is firm. Handsome and brave though you are, you will never succeed in winning her love.'

Udayakumaran caught sight of Manimekalai reflected through the crystal walls of the pavilion. He was overcome yet again by the sight of her, and heard little of what Sudhamati said to him. He paced up and down, searching for the entrance to the pavilion. When he couldn't find it, he turned to Sudhamati and said, 'I have heard your words, but they have left my feelings for Manimekalai unchanged. I will speak to Chitrapati and ask her to intervene on my behalf.'

Udayakumaran swung into his waiting chariot and left.

Manimekalai heard him and was offended. 'He takes my spiritual beliefs lightly, thinking my affections to be easily bought,' she thought. 'Yet, angry though this makes me, I watch him depart with mixed feelings. My heart reaches out to hold on to him. If this is love then I am better rid of its power!'

Just then, the Goddess Manimekalai Devi, after whom Manimekalai had been named, arrived at the crystal pavilion to worship at the Buddha's feet. Seeing Sudhamati's glum face she asked her what the matter was. Sudhamati briefed her about the day's events.

'It is evident that Udayakumaran intends to pursue this young girl no matter how much she tries to dissuade him. Do not go into the streets of Puhar tonight. Instead, escape into the Chakkaravala Kottam, the cremation ground beyond this garden, and spend the night there in safety,' advised the goddess as she departed.

Sudhamati and Manimekalai entered the Chakkaravala Kottam and fell asleep. Quietly, the Goddess returned, lifted Manimekalai and transported her to the distant island of Manipallavam.

Then Manimekalai Devi returned to Puhar and appeared in a dream to Udayakumaran. 'O Prince,' she said, 'You are the leader of your people. Their well-being should be your main concern. If you continue to pursue Manimekalai, your unrighteous conduct will lead to drought and famine in your kingdom. Give up your love for her and let her proceed on her chosen path in peace.'

Finally, she came back to Sudhamati and woke her. 'The time has come for Manimekalai to begin her quest for salvation. I have taken her to Manipallavam, a place of purity and innocence. There her former life will be revealed to her. She will return to you and Madhavi in seven days.' Manimekalai Devi disappeared, and Sudhamati hurried home to Madhavi.

In Manipallavam, Manimekalai awoke to white, endless sands about her and the gentle music of the sea in her ears. Recognising nothing, she called desperately for Sudhamati but received no reply. She wandered desolately around the island. Then she came upon a beautiful shrine, radiant with light and divine energy. Inside it was the imprint of the holy feet of the Buddha.

Overcome, Manimekalai fell to her knees before the Lord, tears of joy flowing from her eyes. In a flash, her previous birth was revealed to her!

Manimekalai had been Lakshmi, the youngest of three daughters of King Ravivanman, and the beloved wife of Prince Rahulan. Her two elder sisters, Virai and Tarai, were Madhavi and Sudhamati, reborn as her mother and her companion.

The instant Manimekalai gained insight into her past birth, the goddess Manimekalai Devi appeared to her once more. 'Lakshmi, I have another story to tell you. Once when you and Rahulan were together in the palace gardens, the holy monk Sadhuchakkaran passed by. Irritated by the interruption, Rahulan asked the monk rudely what he was doing there. You, on the other hand, bowed before the monk, recognising him as a great disciple of Buddha. You requested that although you were not his follower, he grant you permission to bring him food. The monk accepted your offer. That good deed brought you back in this life as one who is destined to walk in the path of the Buddha and find salvation.

'Your beloved husband Rahulan is none other than Prince Udayakumaran. Your devotion to him and the deep love you shared in your previous life will inevitably draw you to each other in this birth. Knowing this, I have taken you away from Puhar, in the hope that the tiny seed of Dharma that was planted in you in your former life will grow and bear fruit, unhindered by physical and emotional attachments.

'Now that you know your former life and understand the nature of Dharma, you must learn more about other religions. However, many teachers will refuse to instruct you, because you are young and also because you are a woman. So here are three mantras. The first will enable you to change your physical form at will. The second will allow you to travel through air. The third will protect you against hunger.'

The goddess instructed Manimekalai on the three mantras until the girl had committed them to memory. After the goddess left, Manimekalai wandered around the island, exploring the beauty of the place. Suddenly a lovely woman hailed her. It was Divatilakai, the patron goddess of the shrine of Buddha.

'Manimekalai,' she said, 'your presence on this island at the time of the annual full moon day of Vaikasi tells me that you are truly the chosen one.'

'Chosen for what, Mother?' asked Manimekalai.

'Child,' replied the goddess, 'every year at Vaikasi, the legendary alms bowl called Amudasurabi that once belonged to Aaputran appears in the Komugi Lake, seeking the hands of its new owner. I believe you are the one it has waited for these many years.'

As the goddess led Manimekalai to the lake, she told her the story of Aaputran ...

'Aaputran's mother abandoned him at birth because he was not her husband's child. A cow, hearing the hungry cries of the infant, lovingly nursed him for many days. Then the childless Brahmin Bhuti found him and adopted him. When Aaputran grew into a young man, he was ostracised by his people for freeing a sacrificial cow. Perhaps in his subconscious there existed a memory of a cow nurturing him like a mother, and the thought of any cow being put to death was intolerable to him.

'Aaputran made his way to the Pandyan Capital of Madurai and wandered the streets, begging. The blind, diseased and destitute beggars in the city shared their food with him. At night he slept outside the temple of Chinta Devi, using his begging bowl as a pillow. One night some travellers came to the temple and asked Aaputran for food. He was broken-hearted that he had so little to share with these hungry people. Witnessing his torment, the Goddess Chinta Devi appeared before him with an alms bowl in her hand, saying, 'Son, take this bowl, the Amudasurabi. Even if this land is plunged in famine, this bowl will never be empty.'

'Aaputran now spent his days in deep contentment, feeding the poor and the hungry. One day, Indra appeared before Aaputran, wanting to reward him for his good deeds. But Aaputran only laughed. "Lord, what reward can bring me greater happiness than I already get from feeding the hungry?" he questioned.

'Indra was mortified. He caused the rains to fall until the dried riverbeds flowed in abundance, crops flourished, and hunger was eradicated from the land. Now Aaputran was left with nothing to do. Dejected at not being able to put to use the wonderful powers of the bowl, he came to the island of Manipallavam and surrendered it to the Lake Komugi. He asked the bowl to appear in that place each year to seek another who might be able to put it to its proper use. Then, on this very island, he gave up his life.'

This was Aaputran's story. The bowl was the Amudasurabi, which found its way into Manimekalai's hands that fateful Vaikasi day ...

Manimekalai returned to Puhar with the bowl. She wore the robes of an ascetic, took the Amudasurabi in her hand and went out into the streets of Puhar. People recognised her and were surprised by her fearlessness in appearing so publicly when Prince Udayakumaran was still searching for her. Unperturbed, Manimekalai walked on, distributing food to the hungry.

Meanwhile, Chitrapati, Madhavi's mother, was outraged
at what she thought her granddaughter had done. It was not
fitting, in her opinion, that one of their profession should
renounce the world. It was for Manimekalai to catch a rich
man with her beauty and dance, get from him all she could,
and then leave him when a better prospect came along. She
vowed to rid Manimekalai of her begging bowl and hand her
over to Udayakumaran!

When she approached him, Chitrapati found
Udayakumaran depressed. He was disturbed by Manimekalai
Devi's warning in his dream. Chitrapati laughed away his
fears saying, 'Manimekalai was born to enjoy men and be
enjoyed by them. Therefore, O prince, you need have no
qualms about seeking her out.' She told him where to find
Manimekalai—at the cosmic shrine called the Ulaga Aravi
inside the Chakkaravala Kottam.

Udayakumaran needed no further encouragement.
He hurried there and saw Manimekalai giving alms to the
unfortunate, hungry souls that roamed the Chakkaravala
Kottam.

'She is feeding so many out of one tiny bowl!' was his first
incredulous thought. Then his heart constricted with pain
and longing. 'How can she enter my heart so thoroughly and
then renounce this world without a thought for what will
become of me?'

Udayakumaran waited until Manimekalai was alone and
went up to her. These were the first words he ever spoke to

her, as he took her hand gently in his and said, 'Tell me your reason for renouncing the world.'

At his touch and the sight of his face, Manimekalai's heart stirred. 'This is my husband from another life,' she thought. 'I must show him respect. And yet, I must overcome my longing for him, for my mission in this lifetime requires me to walk a path that is different from his.'

Quietly withdrawing her hand she said, 'I have understood that the body is a vessel of attachment, disease, sorrow and pain. In order to break away from this body and this earthly world of never-ending desires, I have chosen to walk the path of dharma, and live the life of a monk.'

She turned and walked into the shrine. Knowing that Udayakumaran would never leave her alone if he saw her again, Manimekalai used the mantra the goddess had taught her and changed herself into Kayachandikai, a beggar woman who was awaiting the return of her husband, from whom she had been separated by a curse. Manimekalai believed this woman to have left Puhar, and so chose to take on her form.

Still reeling from Manimekalai's softly uttered words, Udayakumaran stood where she had left him. A few minutes later he saw Kayachandikai emerge. He walked up to the goddess of the shrine and said, 'You have hidden my love from me. But I will find her and take her away from here. This is a vow I make at your feet.'

To his surprise the goddess herself addressed him. 'Your vow is meaningless. Manimekalai is not to be swayed from her chosen path. What you hope for will never come to pass. Therefore remove her from your heart and go in peace.'

Fresh in his memory was the warning uttered by the goddess Manimekalai Devi in his dream. Moreover, he had seen with his own eyes the miracle performed by the alms bowl in Manimekalai's hands. Now the goddess in this temple had spoken to him. Confused, torn between what was apparent and the dictates of his heart, Udayakumaran decided to keep a close watch on his beloved and choose his future course of action based on what he observed. Bowing to the deity, he returned to the palace.

Manimekalai, disguised as Kayachandikai, made her way to the town prison. With the Amudasurabi, she tended to the prisoners who were suffering inside. The prison guards were astonished by what they saw and hurried to the king. When they were granted an audience they cried, 'Your Majesty, the beggar Kayachandikai entered the prison and fed all the prisoners out of a single bowl of alms!'

The king asked to meet this young woman. When Manimekalai was summoned, he asked her who she was.

'Take me to be the person I appear to be, Your Majesty—a beggar woman forced to wander the streets. I have fed the people with the aid of this miraculous bowl.'

'Pious maiden, ask me for anything and I will grant it to you,' said the king, touched by the girl's simplicity.

'Then free all the prisoners, O king, and let that place cease to be a house of sorrow. Instead let it become a Buddhist monastery.'

'So be it,' said the King, and Manimekalai went on her way.

Before long, Udayakumaran heard of this encounter. He was overcome with a suspicion that the so-called Kayachandikai, who had appeared from the Ulaga Aravi in place of Manimekalai with the same alms bowl in her hands, was none other than Manimekalai. Determined to find out the truth, he made straight for the Ulaga Aravi.

As luck would have it, Kanjanan, the husband of Kayachandikai, was also headed for the same place in search of his wife. He reached the Ulaga Aravi just before Udayakumaran did. He eagerly approached Manimekalai, mistaking her for his beloved Kayachandikai. But when he spoke to her she paid him no heed, for she had ears only for the voice of the hungry.

When, moments later, she saw Udayakumaran, she approached him and spoke to him in low tones.

'Look about you, O Prince. Look upon hunger, disease and old age, the seeds of which exist in even the most beautiful of bodies. Understand the transience of youth and beauty, and release yourself from their binding power,' she counselled.

Instead of convincing him, Manimekalai's words only served to confirm in Udayakumaran's mind what he had already guessed. This young woman was none other than his beloved! He turned and walked away, intending to return in the night and confront Manimekalai alone. Kanjanan was outraged.

His wife had ignored him and openly sought the company of another man! He hid himself and bided his time.

In the dead of night, Udayakumaran approached the shrine of the Ulaga Aravi. Manimekalai was inside, praying. Before Udayakumaran could enter, Kanjanan, swift as a cobra, withdrew his sword and struck the prince dead! Alarmed, the goddess cried out, 'Kanjanan, you have made a terrible mistake! The woman inside is Manimekalai, disguised as your wife. The real Kayachadikai has gone away to search for you.'

Horrified by the enormity of his crime, Kanjanan fled the kingdom.

Manimekalai heard the goddess and came running. When she saw Udayakumaran lying dead upon the temple steps, she found it difficult to control her grief.

'O Prince,' she murmured, 'I had hoped to share with you the truths I had learnt. But I took on the form of Kayachandikai to do so, and this has led to your death!' And she changed herself back to her original form.

As she approached Udayakumaran's lifeless body, the goddess of the shrine called out once more, 'Do not go near him! Do not touch him! It is not only in your former life, but also in many other lifetimes before, that he has been your husband. So your love for him is natural. But if you are ever to break away from him who is your strongest attachment, you must walk away now and put aside all grief. Else you will have to be reborn to break your bond with Udayakumaran once again.'

'I will do as you say,' said Manimekalai. 'But tell me why the prince has met with such a vicious end. What actions of his have brought this on?'

The goddess replied, 'When you, Lakshmi, and your husband Rahulan intended to take food for the holy monk, one of the cooks arrived late. In his hurry to get the meal ready on time, he tripped over a vessel of rice, defiling it. Angered, Rahulan severed the man's head with his sword. That action has carried into this lifetime and he has paid the price.'

Hearing these words, Manimekalai's grief lessened, and she became calm.

The goddess then warned Manimekalai in advance of what was soon to befall her at the hands of Queen Seerthi, Udayakumaran's mother. Manimekalai thanked the goddess for her advice and went her way.

The next morning, the sadhus of the Chakkaravala Kottam brought the news of Udayakumaran's death to the king. They showed him how, in pursuing a chaste woman who had chosen the path of renunciation, the prince had done wrong and brought about his own death. The pious king, grieved though he was, put aside his sorrow and said, 'Kanjanan was wrong to kill my son. But through his mistake he brought justice to the prince where, I, as king, should have done the deed. Prepare the prince for cremation.'

Queen Seerthi was beside herself. However, she concealed the bitterness and intense emotions that she felt and bid her time for revenge against Manimekalai, who she was convinced was the cause of her son's death. She said to the king, 'My lord, allow me to bring Manimekalai into the palace and protect her against others who, like our son, may try to hamper her spiritual progress.'

So Manimekalai was summoned to the palace, where she was made to live. The Queen planned to poison her until she lost her mind, and then turn her into the streets to be stoned and ridiculed by the townspeople. But forewarned by the goddess of the temple, Manimekalai consumed the poison and remained in full possession of her senses.

Next the queen sent a hoodlum into Manimekalai's chambers to molest her. Manimekalai transformed herself into a man with the help of the goddess' mantra, and the hoodlum was sent packing. Finally the queen confined her to a single room and denied her food for many weeks. Manimekalai used the third mantra that Manimekalai Devi had taught her to protect herself from hunger. Thus she went about her work cheerfully, unaffected by starvation.

At long last, queen Seerthi realised that this was no ordinary girl. Filled with remorse, she fell at Manimekalai's feet and begged her forgiveness. Manimekalai gently told her about Udayakumaran's previous birth and the action that had led to his brutal end in this life. Thus she brought some measure of understanding and comfort to the distraught mother. Then she took leave of the queen and continued on her way.

Manimekalai reached the island of Java. Aaputran, the original owner of the Amudasurabi, had been reborn as the son of a cow and adopted by Bhumichandran, the king of Java. The king had named the child Puniyarajan, who had grown up to take over the reigns of the kingdom from his father. It was in the hope of meeting him that Manimekalai had come here.

When she landed she was told that since the birth of the prince, the land had known only prosperity and happiness. Disease, drought and famine had become things of the past. Just then Puniyarajan himself arrived with his entourage. When he saw Manimekalai, he was curious. 'Who is this beautiful girl who has become an ascetic at such a young age?' he asked.

His minister, who had seen Manimekalai and heard much of her during his travels abroad, told the king about her. Even as he spoke, Manimekalai stepped forward.

'O king, this is the bowl that once belonged to you.'

Puniyarajan was puzzled. Seeing incomprehension on his face she said, 'I see you have forgotten your previous life of generosity and goodness. But surely you are aware of the unusual circumstances of your birth in this life?'

Puniyarajan was speechless, for he believed himself to be the real son of Bhumichandran.

'Then you must travel to Manipallavam. There, at the shrine of the Buddha, you will come to know of the events of your previous birth,' instructed Manimekalai, and left.

The king hurried home to the Queen Mother. When he questioned her about his birth she revealed to him how he had been born of a cow and later adopted by Bhumichandran.

'How strange,' thought Puniyarajan. 'I am still king of this land, and yet everything has changed. My desire for material pleasures, so strong till a few moments ago, has gone completely. I will do as that girl told me and go to Manipallavam.'

At Manipallavam he found Manimekalai waiting for him, her face alight with a smile of welcome. She took him to the shrine of the Buddha where he saw, in a blinding flash, the worthy and beautiful life that Aaputran had led. He came to know that the soul of Aaputran was the very one that now belonged to him.

At that moment the goddess Divatilakai appeared. 'O king,' she said, 'it is here that the pious Aaputran gave up his life. You have returned to the land where the remains of your body from your previous life now lie buried under sand.'

Puniyarajan dropped to his knees. He parted the layers of sand until he uncovered a pile of bones—all that was left of Aaputran's body! He was shaken by this visible proof of the transience of life. 'Then this world is impermanent,' he thought. 'Only the soul and its actions outlive death.'

Manimekalai watched him compassionately. 'Why are you sad? Though Aaputran is dead, his soul and his goodness live on in you. I brought you here to understand this. Now return to your land and rule your people with love and generosity.'

'No,' replied Puniyarajan. 'I wish to choose your path, the path of renunciation.'

'Your desire for it is enough to ensure that in your next life you will get the chance to do so. But for now, great king, your dharma is to rule. You have a duty to your people. If you turn your face away from it, you will be acting against your dharma.'

Understanding her words, Puniyarajan bowed to this great soul and went back to Java. Manimekalai proceeded to Vanji, the Chera capital.

Disguised as an old mendicant scholar, Manimekalai entered Vanji. There she spent many months with great and learned men, listening to all they had to teach her about their different religions. They freely opened their hearts to her, believing her to be a man in pursuit of truth. In the end nothing any of them told her could satisfactorily answer her questions on what true Dharma was. She moved on until she came to the holy city of Kanchi, laid to waste by a terrible famine. Manimekalai fed the starving from her alms-bowl, like a mother feeds her hungry children. When everybody had eaten and the last of them had departed, Manimekalai looked up from her task and saw Sage Aravana Adigal, accompanied by Madhavi and Sudhamati.

Overjoyed, she ran to the sage and bowed to him. When she had recounted all her experiences and all that she had learned, Aravana Adigal smiled.

'Child, I see that the time has now come for me to initiate you into the path of salvation.'

The great sage revealed to her the secret of Dharma and taught her how to free her soul from the cycle of birth and death. Then, his work complete, Aravana Adigal turned and walked away. Manimekalai never saw him again.

Manimekalai lived the rest of her life in piety and goodness, Madhavi and Sudhamati by her side. This beautiful girl from the street of dancers and courtesans went on to become one of Lord Buddha's chief disciples.

Urubhangam

Bhasa

The story goes like this. Five brothers lost their kingdom to a hundred in a game of dice. In keeping with the conditions of the game, the losers went into exile, spending the thirteenth and final year in hiding.

Their banishment complete, the five brothers returned to find that their kingdom was still not to be handed back to them. Instead, they would have to fight a war—among the greatest and bloodiest ever—to wrest back their kingdom. On one side of the battlefield stood their grand uncle, their teacher, their hundred cousins and other stalwarts, backed by a formidable army.

On the other side stood the five brothers, their courage...and Krishna.

Within the main body of the story run a myriad smaller ones. The playwright Bhasa wrote six of them—his version of what happened between the Kauravas and the Pandavas in this great epic.

Bhasa lived and wrote in the fourth century BC, *some hundred years before Kalidasa. Two thousand years later, he is still celebrated as one of the greatest playwrights in history.*

The story that follows is a compilation of six short plays. They follow the sequential order of the original story even though they do not tell a continuous tale.

The first play, The Middle One, *is about the meeting between the Pandava Bheem Sena and Ghatotkacha, his son through the ogress Hidimba. It is interesting to note that the original epic has no such meeting.*

Five Nights *is based on a well-known episode in the* Mahabharata, *but with an interesting twist lent to the story by the playwright. He gives a new motive to the capture of king Virat's cattle by the Kuru army. Bhasa has also deviated from the original characterisations of the protagonists. Bheeshma, the grandsire, is a crafty old fellow, and Dhronacharya, the guru, is a bit of a simpleton.*

The last of the six plays is Urubhangam, *which translates to 'the shattered thigh'. By the end of this, the final play, Bhasa leaves no doubt in the minds of his audience that he considers Duryodhana to be the real hero of the* Mahabharata.

In Bhasa's time, the death of a character was only depicted through words, and plays always ended on a happy note. The enactment of the heart-rending death of Duryodhana in Urubhangam *is an interesting breach of the traditions of dramaturgy of that era.*

The Shattered Thigh

The old priest Keshav Das was the first to sense danger. Already apprehensive about passing through the forest at this dark hour with his family, he felt a sudden sharp spasm of fear. He spun around. There it was, a dark shadow, larger than life, looming in the thicket!

'Who are you, sir? Make your presence known!' he cried nervously.

His wife gripped his arm. The three sons instinctively stepped forward to shield their parents. From the thick undergrowth emerged ...

'What is this creature? His hair glows like the sun even in the darkness. His chest is like a lion's. His eyes are as bright as two planets. His face is a great, dark rain cloud and his teeth gleam from behind it like the crescent moon!' cried the second son.

'I am Ghatotkacha, son of the ogress Hidimba,' said the stranger, bowing before the priest.

Keshav Das raised a tremulous hand in blessing. But in his heart he knew they were doomed.

'Good sir,' said Ghatotkacha, 'I know that priests on this earth must be revered. Yet a son's duty to his mother is foremost. Hence, it is with reluctance that I request you to come with me. It is time for my mother's dinner and you shall be so kind as to satisfy her hunger this evening.'

Ghatotkacha stood aside respectfully. He was embarrassed by what he had to do, yet firm that his mother must be fed.

'Why do you look so resigned? Surely we can shout for help?' whispered Keshav Das' wife anxiously.

'From whom, Mother? This place is filled with ogres, and is fit only for hermits,' said the first son.

'Hermits, did you say? Then I might yet be saved! The Pandava hermitage cannot be far from here,' said Keshav Das in relief. 'They are brave warriors and they protect the helpless. They will surely teach this wicked fellow a lesson.'

'But Father,' interjected the first son, 'I don't think the Pandavas are here. I heard that they have left to attend a sacrifice at the hermitage of sage Dhaumya.'

'Not all of them,' said the middle son. 'Bheema, the middle one of the three sons of Kunti has stayed behind to protect the hermitage.'

'His might is equal to all the other four put together!' said Keshav Das.

'But he usually goes to some other part of the forest at this time looking for sport,' said the first son despairingly.

'Then we have no hope, unless ...' said Keshav Das.

'Unless what?' urged his wife.

'Unless I appeal to this fellow. But he is an ogre. How can one expect kindness from him? Still, this is a matter of life or death. Let me at least try, for I have nothing to lose.'

Turning to Ghatotkacha he said humbly, 'Sir, wouldn't it be possible to just let me go?'

Ghatotkacha replied, 'If one of your sons is willing to come with me in your place then the rest of you may leave in peace.'

'Oh, this is cruel!' cried Keshav Das. 'I am a priest, a man of God. How can I abandon a son in his prime of life to a man-eating demon like you?'

'Sir, if you will not surrender one member of your family to me then I will be forced to take you all,' said Ghatotkacha unrelentingly.

'Then here is my decision,' said the priest. 'I am old and have lived my life. I will come with you. Only, spare my sons.'

'No!' cried the wife. 'How can I, a devoted wife, live without you? Let me go with him.' The poor lady's words were brave, but the tremor in her voice, the terror in her eyes betrayed her.

'Madam, I cannot take you. My mother does not want a woman.'

'Father, let me go,' pleaded the first son. 'I wish to give up my life to save those of my parents and younger brothers.'

'No brother, I should go,' protested the middle son. 'You are the eldest and therefore most important to this family.'

'When the father is in difficulty it is the duty of the eldest son to ease it,' said the first.

'But how can I bear to let you go? You, my eldest son, the apple of my eye?' said Keshav Das.

'Then I will go,' declared the third son.

'No!' cried the mother, putting out her hand in a frightened way. 'You are my youngest and are dearest to me.'

'Then the choice is made,' said the middle son with satisfaction. 'I am the middle son, the least favoured. My death will cause the least grief.' Turning to Ghatotkacha he said, 'Sir, will my going with you be acceptable to you?'

'It will,' replied Ghatotkacha.

The middle one bowed to his distraught parents, securing their blessings. Next he embraced his two brothers. Turning once again to Ghatotkacha he requested to be allowed to quench his thirst at the nearby lake.

'Go, but hurry back, please. It is almost time for my mother's meal.'

The middle one disappeared into the trees. The water might merely have been an excuse. Perhaps he needed a few minutes alone, poor lad, to prepare for death, away from his unhappy family.

After he had gone, the old priest knelt down and wept. 'Oh my child, so brave, so beautiful. You go to your death hiding your fear so that I may be spared the added pain of witnessing your turmoil.'

'Sir,' interrupted Ghatotkacha gently after some minutes, 'It is getting late. Your son has still not returned. Please summon him.'

Keshav Das raised imploring eyes to Ghatotkacha. 'How can you be so cruel as to ask me to summon my child to his own death?'

'Be patient with me, O priest. I mean no unkindness. An ogre's natural food is man. I am only acting in accordance with my nature.' Turning to the first son Ghatotkacha said, 'Please tell me your brother's name. I will call him myself.'

'We call him Madhyama, the middle one.'

Raising his voice Ghatotkacha called, 'Madhyama! O Madhyama, come quickly.'

Bheema, the middle brother of the Pandavas, happened to be in those parts at that moment. Used to being addressed by the same title, he immediately responded, 'Who calls me in a voice so like Arjuna's?' He stepped into the clearing where the priest and the others stood.

When he came face to face with Ghatotkacha, Bheema was struck by his regal bearing and formidable looks. 'Clearly the son of some powerful warrior,' he thought, not recognising this son whom he had parted from at birth.

At the same moment Ghatotkacha was thinking, 'What a handsome man! His arms are like columns, his shoulders glisten like Garuda's wings, his eyes glow like blue lotuses. Why do I feel drawn to him, as if he were a long lost kinsman?' Aloud he said, 'Sir, are you also the middle one?'

'My brothers call me Madhyama, yes. I am one of five exiled brothers, the wind among the five elements.'

Keshav Das gave a start. 'Exiled brothers?' he thought. 'The wind? This is beyond a doubt the great Pandava Bheema, son of Vayu. We are saved!'

At that moment, the priest's middle son returned from the lake.

'Ah, you are the middle one I wanted,' said Ghatotkacha. 'Come, my mother must not be kept waiting any longer.'

'No!' cried Keshav Das. Turning quickly to Bheema he poured out his story, begging him to save his family.

'This priest is like the moon with three stars. Why do you wish to eclipse them?' asked Bheema of Ghatotkacha. 'According to Hindu dharma, priests are not harmed even if they commit crimes, whereas these people are innocent. Leave them in peace and go on your way.'

'No,' replied Ghatotkacha, respectfully but firmly.

'This brave and strong-willed youth possesses all the qualities of my four brothers. In might he is my equal. His disposition calls to mind that of Abhimanyu. Whose son could he be?' thought Bheema, deeply impressed in spite of his irritation. Aloud he said, 'You will do as I say.'

'Indeed sir, even if my father were to order me to do so I would not obey him. For I take this priest's son on the express command of my mother.'

Bheema frowned. 'Who is your mother?'

'The ogress Hidimba. She is married to the great Pandava Bheema.'

'Then he is my son!' thought Bheema with a start, a surge of love and pride filling his heart. However he revealed nothing to the others. At his lack of response to Ghatotkacha's declaration, Keshav Das began to doubt whether he was indeed Bheema the Pandava. If this man was not Bheema then he would never be able to vanquish the ogre in battle. Keshav Das' heart sank again.

Then Bheema said to Ghatotkacha, 'Leave this young man and take me instead.'

'Sir,' cried the second son of the priest, 'I cannot allow you to do any such thing. You are brave and in your prime. Your place is on earth. I have already surrendered my life to this ogre. Let me go with him.'

'It is the duty of a Kshatriya to protect others, especially Brahmins,' said Bheema. Turning to Keshav Das he said, 'Please take your wife and three sons and be on your way.'

'You speak like a warrior. Aren't you afraid of me? I will kill you and take the second son. There is nobody here to stop me,' said Ghatotkacha.

'I will stop you,' Bheema assured him calmly.

'Then follow me and prepare to fight.'

'I follow only those who are stronger than I am. You will have to take me by force.'

'Do you know who I am?' cried Ghatotkacha, goaded by the lack of fear in Bheema's voice.

'You are my son.'

'What?' scoffed Ghatotkacha. 'How am I your son?'

'Forgive me,' said Bheema gently 'We warriors refer to everybody as our son. Hence I addressed you in the same way.'

'From the way you speak sir, you sound less like a warrior than a coward.'

Bheema smiled. 'I don't know the meaning of fear. I was born without that faculty. Perhaps you can instruct me in it.'

'I will,' said Ghatotkacha, 'And when I am done you will never forget it. Take up your weapons, sir.'

'I hold my weapon,' said Bheema, indicating his right arm.

'Only my father, the mighty Bheema, has the right to speak in such a manner.'

'Who is this cowardly Bheema? Is he the god of creation, the god of death or the king of heaven, that you speak of him so highly?'

'He compares with them all,' replied Ghatotkacha.

'Surely you exaggerate,' replied Bheema, amused at the irony of the situation and Ghatotkacha's earnestness.

Believing Bheema to be scorning his father, Ghatotkacha was outraged. He uprooted a tree and lashed out at him.

'But he remains unharmed!' thought Ghatotkacha in surprise. 'I will strike him again! And again!' With a roar, Ghatotkacha began to lash out at Bheema with the tree trunk, over and over again.

Bheema stood laughing under these heavy blows. Abandoning the tree, Ghatotkacha grasped Bheema with his mighty arms, intending to wrestle him to death. Bheema moved quick as lightning and twisted Ghatotkacha's arms into an unbreakable lock.

Gasping, helpless, Ghatotkacha grew desperate. 'Remember your promise!' he cried, as a last resort.

'That I remember well,' replied Bheema, releasing him. 'I will go with you to your mother like I pledged to.'

'I will go and inform her that you are coming.' He started in the direction of his home when suddenly he stopped and peered amongst the trees. 'Wait, no need for that. She approaches herself. Greetings, mother. Your dinner awaits you.'

Hidimba stepped into the clearing, a tall and handsome woman. When she saw Bheema, her eyes widened with joy.

Not observing his mother's reaction to the stranger Ghatotkacha added, 'You will be more than pleased with your prey, for he is neither an old man nor a child. He is a man whose power is far greater than a mere mortal's.'

'You idiot, he is no man,' cried Hidimba. 'He is God!'

'God?' questioned Ghatotkacha, puzzled, looking from one to the other.

'Yes, *our* god. This is the mighty Pandava Bheem Sena, my husband and your father!'

Overcome by horror at how he had treated his father, yet thrilled at this unexpected meeting, Ghatotkacha fell to his knees before Bheema, saying, 'Father, I bow to you. Forgive me for my mistake, it was committed in ignorance.'

Clasping his valiant son to his breast, Bheema murmured, 'You are forgiven a thousand times over! Only the fortunate are blessed with sons like you. Live on my son, live long!'

Soon after Bheema's fateful meeting with Ghatotkacha, the Pandavas' twelfth year in exile came to an end. According to the rules of the game of dice they had lost to the Kauravas, their thirteenth and final year was to be spent in hiding. Bidding goodbye to Hidimba and Ghatotkacha, Bheema and his brothers, along with their wife Draupadi, left the forest and proceeded to the kingdom of Virat, King of

Matsya. There, Bheema, disguised as a cook, served in the royal kitchens. Yudhishtira, under the name of Bhagwan, became the king's companion; Arjuna masquerading as the eunuch Brihannala, taught dance to princess Uttara; Nakul and Sahdev worked in the king's stables.

Meanwhile, in the Kuru court, Dronacharya sat beside Bheeshma, awaiting Duryodhana's arrival. All of them were happy with the success of the sacrifice that Duryodhana had just performed.

Light of step, Duryodhana entered his court, his wily uncle Shakuni, king of Gandhar, not far behind him. 'Gurudev! I bow to you,' he said, prostrating himself before Dronacharya.

'Live long and rule in glory. May you conquer anger and be kind to your kinsmen,' Dronacharya blessed him.

'Ah, preceptor, you hint at the Pandavas when you speak of kinsmen. On the one hand you bless this king's rule, on the other you wish for his throne to pass into the hands of another,' reproached Shakuni.

'Why must you always instigate discord, Shakuni? I wish for Duryodhana to rule fairly. If that means him sharing this kingdom with its rightful heirs, so be it.'

Meanwhile Duryodhana had turned to Karna, his dearest friend, the king of Anga. Embracing him warmly, he received his good wishes. Then he went on to receive the greetings of all the other kings who had travelled from far and near to congratulate him.

'Where is king Virat?' asked Duryodhana. 'Only he seems to be missing from this august gathering.'

'I have sent an emissary to him. Perhaps he is on his way,' replied Shakuni.

'Gurudev, you are the preceptor. I owe the success of this sacrifice, as I do every other success, to you. Please accept the fee due to you,' said Duryodhana, bowing once again to Dronacharya.

Seeing Dronacharya hesitate and glance at Bheeshma, Duryodhana urged, 'Command me, sir. Everything I have is yours already.'

Dronacharya lowered his eyes.

'Have I done something wrong, Gurudev?' questioned Duryodhana anxiously. Then the truth dawned on him. 'You are thinking of the Pandavas and what you consider my wrongs against them,' he said sadly. Hearing his tone, Shakuni grew worried and took a step closer to him, wanting to intervene if his nephew, in a fit of generous remorse, should make any rash promises.

'Take my hand in yours, Gurudev, and consider it a promise that I will do anything you ask me to,' said Duryodhana softly.

'I believe that you mean well, my son. Then this is the fee I ask—call the homeless Pandavas back and give them their half of the kingdom. If you do this I will feel justly compensated,' said Dronacharya.

'Wait a minute, sir!' cried Shakuni heatedly. 'You are this boy's preceptor. His interest should come first in your heart. How then can you ask him, and on a day like this, to give up something so precious? Is this not trickery in the name of duty?'

'Only your wicked mind could perceive duplicity in my request, Shakuni. What is wrong with brothers sharing their rightful inheritance instead of waging war over it?' asked Dronacharya.

'What you were hoping for and what you got, O sage,' spoke Bheeshma in disgust. 'Let go of your request. Better war than grovelling at the feet of Shakuni.'

But Dronacharya tried again. 'Son, they are weak, homeless, and humbly seek your friendship.'

'I wish to have an opinion on this,' said Duryodhana.

'Whose will you have?' asked Dronacharya excitedly, a glimmer of hope entering his heart. 'The grandsire's? Karna's? Vidura's? Ashwatthama's? Your parents'?'

'My uncle's.'

'No!' groaned Dronacharya, and Bheeshma closed his eyes in despair.

'My opinion is this, my nephew. There will be no sharing of the kingdom,' said Shakuni decisively.

'But uncle, I have given my word to my guru. How can I go back on it?' asked Duryodhana.

'Let me handle this,' replied Shakuni in an undertone. Aloud he said, 'Preceptor, Duryodhana will comply with your request.'

All those present looked up in surprise.

'Only,' continued Shakuni with an insincere smile, 'We have a condition.'

'Of course,' said Bheeshma. 'Under your tutelage, Shakuni, every gift will doubtless come with conditions.'

'What is the condition?' asked Dronacharya resignedly.

'If the Pandavas, who are now in hiding, can be discovered within five nights, they shall have half the kingdom as you requested.'

Dronacharya frowned, uncomprehending. 'But you will make no efforts towards finding them and I will lose the condition.'

'Ah, but the onus of discovering them lies with *you*, preceptor,' said Shakuni cunningly.

'If you couldn't find them these last twelve years with all your trickery, then how am I to find them in five nights?' asked Dronacharya.

Just then an envoy arrived.

'Victory to the king! I bring news from Matsya. King Virat is mourning his dead relatives and hence cannot come.'

'What happened?' asked Shakuni.

'Sir, his cousins, the hundred Keechaka brothers, were secretly slain in the dead of night by one man with his bare hands.'

Bheeshma gave a start. 'With bare hands, you say? How can you be so sure?'

'Sir, there was not a trace on their bodies that any weapons had been used.'

In a whisper, Bheeshma urged Dronacharya, 'Accept Shakuni's challenge at once, O sage. We have found the Pandavas.'

'What do you mean?' asked Dronacharya.

'Only Bheema could have murdered a hundred mighty Keechakas with his bare hands!'

Seeing the truth in his words Dronacharya turned to Duryodhana and said, 'My son, in all this confusion I never told you my decision. I accept your challenge. I will find the Pandavas in five nights. Are you sure you will comply with your promise if I should succeed?'

Taken aback, Duryodhana said, 'I will.'

Acting quickly Bheeshma said, 'Be that as it may, let us first deal with the news this envoy has brought us from Matsya. Duryodhana, I'm afraid this excuse of being in mourning is only a fabrication. In fact Virat has a deep and hidden enmity with me and has chosen this way to insult us. We must retaliate.'

'O Bheeshma, how can you say this? Virat is a true well-wisher of ours!' protested a distressed Dronacharya.

'Don't you understand that the sound of the battle cry will surely draw the Pandavas out of hiding?' replied Bheeshma in a low voice.

'How do we punish them, Grandfather?' asked Duryodhana not hearing the exchange between his grandfather and his teacher.

'Seize their cattle. King of Gandhar, Shakuni, would you like to lead the expedition?'

The request pleased Shakuni very much. He lost no time in capturing the cattle and herding them away. As predicted by Bheeshma, the Pandavas rallied around Virat when the news reached the court of Matsya. Heading out to rescue the cattle was king Virat's son Uttar, with none other than Brihannala as his charioteer! They set out for the battlefield with a sizable army. When they arrived, the sight of the formidable Kuru warriors scared Uttar so badly that he lost his nerve and hastily commanded Brihannala to retreat.

But Arjuna never turned his face away from battle. He was incapable of it. Taking matters into his own hands, he changed places with Uttar and wreaked terror on the Kuru army, rescued the cattle and returned to Matsya victorious! Meanwhile Bheema, who had gone to the war still disguised as a cook, strolled up to Abhimanyu's chariot, lifted him out and brought him back to the court of king Virat. Abhimanyu, son of Arjuna and Subhadra, had been fighting on the side of the Kurus. He was outraged at this indignity!

At the court of king Virat a messenger came bursting in.

'Victory to the king!'

'What news? You appear excited.'

'Your Majesty, Abhimanyu has been taken prisoner by your cook!'

Brihannala and Bhagwan glanced at each other joyfully. 'Then he was not captured,' thought Brihannala. 'I was content to look upon my son from afar. But Bheema couldn't contain himself. He went ahead and embraced the boy!'

'Bring him in with due honours. Because of my relationship with Bheeshma, the boy is like my grandson,' said the king.

Abhimanyu, accompanied by Bheema, entered the court. Unable to contain himself any longer, Brihannala stepped forward with shining eyes and said, 'Abhimanyu, how are you?'

'Abhimanyu? Do low people take the name of princes in these parts? Is that the custom here?' But privately the boy's thoughts were, 'A woman's ornaments are out of place on this person. Such a manly body, such a noble air, not unlike a god.'

'I have angered him,' said Brihannala quietly to Bheema. 'You make him speak, for I long to hear him.'

'How is your mother?' asked Bheema gently.

'Are you my fathers Yudhishtira, Bheema or Arjuna that you dare to inquire after the ladies of our family?' demanded Abhimanyu, outraged.

Suddenly Bhagwan laughed. 'We are your fathers, son. I am Yudhishtira. The man who brought you here is Bheema, and that is Arjuna.' Glancing quickly at his aghast brothers, he added, 'It is okay—today our final year in exile has expired.'

Realisation dawned on Virat, Abhimanyu and all the others present. Throwing himself at their feet, Abhimanyu begged his fathers to forgive his rudeness. King Virat said heartily, 'It is my honour that the Pandavas chose my home to spend their final year of exile in. If I have unknowingly wronged you, I humbly beg your forgiveness.'

Then King Virat offered Arjuna the hand of his daughter Uttara in marriage. Arjuna declined. 'As my student she occupies the place of a daughter in my heart. Let her marry my son Abhimanyu and take her rightful place in my home.'

Overjoyed, King Virat accepted.

Meanwhile, in the court of Duryodhana, a chamberlain brought the news of Abhimanyu's capture. Startled, Duryodhana said, 'Then we must liberate him at once! My differences are with his fathers, but he is like my own child. We must act fast.'

'Surely Virat will release him soon enough for fear of Arjuna's anger and Krishna's and Balarama's,' dismissed Shakuni uncaringly.

Suddenly Duryodhana noticed that neither Bheeshma nor Dronacharya appeared too concerned by the news of Abhimanyu's capture. 'Indeed, they look positively triumphant,' he thought. 'How can that be? Abhimanyu is the apple of their eye.'

'Gurudev, what is it?' he questioned.

'Son, I believe I have won the bet we had taken.'

'How so?' demanded Shakuni.

'We have found the Pandavas.'

'Indeed, no. For where are they? You would have to present them,' said Shakuni.

Turning to the chamberlain, Dronacharya commanded, 'Show us one of those deadly arrows that were supposedly released from Uttar's bow.'

The chamberlain left the court and returned with an arrow.

'What is going on?' asked Duryodhana, confused. But a look of fear had entered Shakuni's eyes. All those present waited with bated breath. Dronacharya took the arrow and examined it carefully. Then he looked up and gave them a radiant smile. 'This is Arjuna's arrow!'

'No!' said Shakuni. But by now it was clear that Dronacharya had spoken the truth.

'Wait. Might not this be the arrow of some other warrior who also bears the same name?' asked Shakuni, grasping at straws.

'I will only concede defeat if I see Yudhishtira at the court of king Virat,' said Duryodhana defiantly.

Hardly had the words left his mouth when a chamberlain entered. 'Sire, an envoy has arrived from the court of Matsya.'

'What does he say?' asked Duryodhana.

'He brings an invitation from King Yudhisthira to the wedding of his son Abhimanyu with the princess of Matsya.'

Duryodhana turned pale and sat down heavily on his throne, unable to utter a word.

'My child,' said Dronacharya gently, 'The truth is before you. Will you keep your promise and hand over half the kingdom to the Pandavas?'

Duryodhana nodded. 'I will, Gurudev,' he said with sincerity, and Bheeshma and Dronacharya sighed with relief, believing that peace had arrived at last ...

But this proved to be merely a delusion.

Goaded by Shakuni, to whose nature peace was abhorrent, Duryodhana went back on his word. When the Pandavas returned from exile, he refused to hand over their share of the kingdom. What ensued was a series of unsuccessful attempts on the part of the Pandavas to regain their share of the kingdom peacefully. Krishna was sent to the Kuru court as an envoy, but he was insulted and sent away. Ghatotkacha was sent to issue a warning that if Duryodhana did not keep his promise he would pay heavily. Ghatotkacha was ridiculed. The Kuru elders—Bheeshma, Drona, Gandhari and Dhritarashtra—all were in favour of a peaceful settlement. They begged and counselled Duryodhana in vain. For Shakuni wielded the greatest influence over him.

And so the battle of Kurukshetra took place.

For eighteen long days the two mighty armies raged and schemed, fought and killed, until all that remained were the five Pandavas and Krishna on one side, and Duryodhana on the other. Now Duryodhana engaged Bheema in battle, the final battle of this dark and bloody war.

The combatants were evenly matched. Both highly skilled with the mace and powerful of body, they fought on until it appeared things would end in an impasse. The only witnesses were Krishna, Balarama and the four other Pandavas.

Although he knew that Duryodhana was in the wrong, Balarama, who had taught him to wield the mace, had a deep affection for him. While his conscience was with Bheema, his heart was with Duryodhana. So when Krishna, impatient for victory, slapped his thigh as a signal to Bheema, Balarama grew alarmed. It was against the rules of war to strike an opponent below the waist. Before he could intervene, Bheema raised his mace and struck Duryodhana on the thigh, shattering it!

The war was over! There was no doubt now that Duryodhana's injury would prove fatal, sooner or later. The Pandavas, accompanied by Krishna, left the battlefield.

'O shame!' cried Balarama. 'They cheated in battle. Duryodhana, my poor friend, I vow that I will present you with Bheema's bloodied and mutilated body.'

Blinded by pain, Duryodhana cried out, 'No, Balarama, let it go. Bheema was only fulfilling his vow. We are finished, the war has ended. Now let the funeral of the Kuru clan proceed. I will be joining my brothers soon.'

Suddenly the sound of voices reached their ears. Turning, Balarama saw Dhritarashtra and Gandhari, accompanied by Pauravi and Malavi, Duryodhana's two wives, and his young son Durjaya, approaching. The old parents were stumbling along as fast as their sightless eyes would allow, desperate to find their eldest, their dearest and last remaining son.

'My child! Where are you? Come to me!' pleaded Dhritarashtra.

Duryodhana tried to haul himself up but fell back helplessly, sudden tears blinding him. 'O Balarama, Bheema's mace has deprived me of the use of my legs as well as the honour of greeting my parents.'

'Where are you, Gandhari?' asked Dhritarashtra.

'I'm here, my lord. Unfortunately still alive,' replied Gandhari bitterly.

'Can you see our child?' asked Dhritarashtra.

'No, my lord, I cannot.'

'O Gandhari, today my sightless eyes have been blinded more than ever by the tears that flow at the news of our son being struck down by treachery.'

Durjaya, Duryodhana's little son, caught sight of his father and ran to him. 'Father, there you are! I have been watching from the palace window for your return. I want to sit in your lap.'

'Durjaya, no!' cried Duryodhana, the pain in his heart mingling with the searing pain in his thigh as Durjaya tried to climb onto it.

'Why won't you let me sit in your lap?' asked Durjaya sadly.

'Sit elsewhere, my son. After today your old sitting place will exist no more.'

Hearing these words, Malavi broke down and wept.

'Why do you weep?' asked Duryodhana gently. 'I have fought my battles with honour, and now I have earned my place in heaven. Beloved, you are the wife of a warrior. It does not suit you to weep.'

'What do I know of war, my lord? I am just a woman, your wife, and hence I weep,' replied Malavi.

'And you Pauravi, you, who have walked by my side these many years, fulfilled family obligations and sacrifices along with me. There should be no room for tears in your eyes.'

'No, my lord. I have no tears. In death, as in life, I have chosen to go with you.'

'Mother,' said Duryodhana. Gandhari stumbled forward and laid her son's head in her lap. 'If I have done even a single good deed in my life, may I be born as your child in every birth.'

'My darling, this is the dearest wish of my heart,' cried Gandhari, holding her child close to her breast as if to ward off death.

Suddenly Ashwatthama, the son of Dronacharya, came rushing in. 'Where is the king of the Kurus? Ah, there he is, struck down by deceit! My friend, I will avenge this!'

'No, Ashwatthama! My condition today is only the fruit of greed and craving. Give up your anger and live in peace.'

'This I cannot do. They have killed all our men by deceit, and now you. It seems along with breaking your thigh they have broken your pride and spirit too, O king. But not mine. I may be the only man standing, but I will fight to the end and win! Durjaya, come to me.'

Placing a hand on the little boy's head, Ashwatthama said, 'I swear on the head of the uncrowned prince of the Kurus that I will kill the Pandavas and Krishna tonight in their sleep. They shall not wake to see the sun.'

'If they have broken my pride then it is well broken. Because of my cursed pride Draupadi was humiliated, the Pandavas were forced into the forest to live with wild beasts, and now their beloved son, Abhimanyu, is dead. What a waste of a beautiful young life! God forgive me!' cried Duryodhana, a spasm of pain and remorse wracking his broken body.

For a long time nobody spoke. Even the wind was silent, and the air still.

'Mother, my life is going,' said Duryodhana at last, quiet now, spent. 'I pass from pain into nothingness, from pride into insignificance, from life into death. I see Shantanu and all my ancestors. They have come to take me with them. Here are my brothers, and Karna, my beloved friend. Here, too, is Abhimanyu, so young, so strong, accusing me of sacrificing his innocent life on the altar of my greed. Here are the oceans and Mother Ganga, come to cleanse me. Death has sent for me. O Mother, I must go ...'

Duryodhana died quietly with his head in his mother's lap, and was at peace at last.

Too tired to weep, Gandhari laid her son's head gently upon the earth and covered him with a shroud.

'This kingdom has swallowed the life of my hundred sons,' said Dhritarashtra brokenly. 'I can't stay here any longer. I must go to the forest and live there until death takes pity on me and reunites me with my children. Gandhari, will you come with me?'

'Anywhere you go, my lord, I will follow.'

The old parents left the battlefield, each laying a hand on little Durjaya's shoulders.

Ashwatthama stood looking sadly down at Duryodhana for a long time. As if gaining determination from the sight of that beloved face, he suddenly turned away saying bitterly, 'I will take up my weapons and go too, ready to kill all those who sleep tonight ...'